THE DRACKENBERG ADVENTURE

BOOKS BY LLOYD ALEXANDER

The Prydain Chronicles

The Book of Three
The Black Cauldron
The Castle of Llyr
Taran Wanderer
The High King

The Westmark Trilogy

Westmark
The Kestrel
The Beggar Queen

The Vesper Holly Adventures

The Illyrian Adventure
The El Dorado Adventure
The Drackenberg Adventure

Other Books for Young People

The First Two Lives of Lukas-Kasha
The Town Cats and Other Tales
The Wizard in the Tree
The Cat Who Wished to Be a Man
The Foundling
The Four Donkeys
The King's Fountain
The Marvelous Misadventures of Sebastian
The Truthful Harp
Coll and His White Pig
Time Cat
Aaron Lopez: The Flagship Hope
August Bondi: Border Hawk
My Five Tigers

THE DRACKENBERG ADVENTURE

LLOYD ALEXANDER

E. P. DUTTON   NEW YORK

Library of Congress Cataloging-in-Publication Data

Alexander, Lloyd.
 The Drackenberg adventure / Lloyd Alexander.
  p. cm.
 Summary: In 1873 seventeen-year-old Vesper Holly and
her guardians travel to an obscure European grand duchy,
where their archenemy Dr. Helvitius is pursuing a lost
art treasure and engineering the country's annexation
by a neighboring kingdom.
 ISBN 0–525–44389–4
 [1. Adventure and adventurers—Fiction.] I. Title.
PZ7.A3774Dr 1988   87–36881
[Fic]—dc19   CIP
                                              AC

Published in the United States by E. P. Dutton,
a division of Penguin Books USA Inc.

Published simultaneously in Canada by
Fitzhenry & Whiteside Limited, Toronto

Editor: Ann Durell
Printed in the U.S.A.   First Edition
10 9 8 7 6 5 4 3 2

for Vespers past, present, and future

THE DRACKENBERG
ADVENTURE

GRAND DUCHY OF DRACKENBERG

DRACKENBERG KOBOLD WOLFBERG

CARLOMANIAN MOUNTAINS

Nymphenbaden
Spa

SOMMERWALD

Gypsy
camp

Schwanfeld
Castle

★ Belgard

Albertine
Palace

KINGDOM OF
← CARPATIA

N
W E
S

Ritterhof
Square

RIVER PRESTA

Map by Meryl Rosner

1

Miss Vesper Holly dislikes weak tea and watercress sandwiches. She avoids those genteel occasions featuring starched collars and white gloves. However, the slightest hint of something out of the ordinary is enough to gain the dear girl's attention.

"When a grand duchess asks you to her diamond jubilee celebration," said Vesper, "that's no tea party invitation. 'The presence of Professor and Mrs. Brinton Garrett is graciously requested. . . .' Brinnie, it's practically a royal command."

We were at breakfast, that autumn day in 1873. The invitation which roused Vesper's curiosity had just arrived in the mail, forwarded to Mary and me at Vesper's mansion in Strafford.

"Her Most Serene Highness Maria-Sophia of Drackenberg." Vesper examined the crested stationery. "She's a friend of yours?"

"Heavens no, child," said Mary. "We have never set

eyes on her. The invitation is merely a courtesy, a polite formality. It is not meant to be accepted."

"Then why send it?" said Vesper.

"Brinnie and I are no doubt on some old official list," Mary answered. "Thanks to my father, very likely. He was in the diplomatic service, and quite highly regarded. He was stationed in Drackenberg some years ago: a place, it would seem, where nobody keeps much of anything up to date, let alone a guest list. No, Her Highness does not expect us to attend. She would be astonished if we did."

"Drackenberg," said Vesper. "I never heard of it."

Nor had most people, I assured her. Like its larger neighbor, Carpatia, the country had fallen, as it were, between the cracks of history. I understood that the capital, Belgard, although handsome and elegant, was outshone by the richer and more glittering attractions of Paris and Vienna. Drackenberg had no valuable resources, no military importance. Even Napoleon, who seldom overlooked an opportunity to enhance his empire, ignored it. As did the rest of the world. Apart from zither music and chicken paprika, Drackenberg offered nothing especially noteworthy. The country was by no means prosperous and had no hope of ever becoming so.

"Still," replied Vesper, "they're bound to do something special to celebrate."

"I am sure they will," said Mary, "whether they can afford it or not. Gala festivals, dances, receptions, grand ceremonies of one sort or another. Yes, it should be most pleasant and eventful."

Mary expressed these remarks in an odd sort of tone. Had I not known her better, I would have called it wistful.

4

Vesper said no more. The dear girl usually attacks her meals exuberantly; now she merely toyed with the grilled salmon. She was, I feared, either ill or deep in thought. Since she has never been sick a day in her life, I concluded it was the latter. Furthermore, her astonishingly green eyes intently concentrated on a point at some distant horizon. I had seen that look before. It should have warned me.

"It's once in a lifetime," said Vesper.

"What's that, dear girl?" I asked.

"A diamond jubilee."

Such, I agreed, was the nature of diamond jubilees.

"What I meant," said Vesper, "was that you and Aunt Mary won't have another chance like this. You really ought to go. The grand duchess invited you, didn't she? Take her up on it."

Of course, it was out of the question. We were much too busy. Vesper's father, my old friend and traveling companion, had named us her guardians. Under the terms of his will, my duties included organizing his journals and personal papers. Dr. Benjamin Rittenhouse Holly, as a brilliant scholar and daring explorer, inspired my admiration. His filing cabinets evoked my despair. I could not possibly interrupt my work, which already promised to be endless.

Mary, always sensible and practical minded, naturally agreed with me. Vesper, who can be insistent in what she believes to be someone's best interests, merely gave a little shrug of disappointment and pursued the subject no further. I considered the matter closed.

It was not.

When Vesper joined us at luncheon, with her orange cat Moggie frisking beside her, she looked in the best of spirits. Her marmalade-colored hair seemed especially vivid, her face shone with an air of happy achievement. I assumed she had successfully completed one of her laboratory experiments.

"About the jubilee," said Vesper. "I accepted for you."

"Dear girl," I cried, "how could you do such a thing?"

"It was easy," said Vesper. "I wrote that you'd be delighted to attend. Come on, Brinnie, you'll complain every minute you're there and have a wonderful time doing it. Besides, I think Aunt Mary's languishing for a holiday."

"My dear child," put in Mary, "I only remarked that it would be a pleasant occasion. I never intended— I'm sure you had our enjoyment at heart. It was lovely and considerate of you. But we cannot simply sail off and leave you. It would be quite irresponsible."

"You're right." Vesper patted Mary's arm. "That's why I'm going with you."

I could not believe my ears. Worse, I could believe them. I gave Mary the opportunity to be the first to protest. To my astonishment, she remained silent.

With Mary obviously dumbstruck by Vesper's announcement, I hurried to speak up for us both. No sooner had I begun than Mary interrupted.

"Brinnie, it is clear to me, whatever the inconveniences, the child must accompany us to Drackenberg. It will be educational and beneficial for her. You should be mindful, my dear Brinnie: It is our first and most solemn

6

duty to help her enlarge her experiences, to make them stimulating and instructive."

To that, I dared not reply. Out of consideration for Mary's delicate and sensitive nature, I had spared her a full account of the details of my previous journeys with Vesper. Heaven forbid she should ever know about Vesper dodging dynamite bombs, galloping through rebel-infested backlands, or confronting earthquakes and volcanic eruptions. For a young woman of seventeen, much less a Philadelphian, Vesper's experiences had already been sufficiently stimulating. As had mine.

Mary's calm gray eyes filled with noble unselfishness. Vesper's smile was just about as innocent as Moggie's. I admitted defeat, perhaps not too gracefully.

And yet, I confess I did not object overstrenuously. If truth were told, I rather looked forward to the prospect of a peaceful—even dull—visit to an obscure corner of the world. In my opinion, dullness has a charm of its own. With Vesper, it would be a novelty.

While the great public festivities would not begin until later in the month, by the time we arrived in Belgard, workmen had started putting up scaffolding along one side of Ritterhof Square. We engaged a somewhat rundown but fairly comfortable suite in a hotel across from the railway terminal. The balcony, at least, would allow us an excellent view of the outdoor celebrations.

Vesper found a bookshop next to a photographer's studio and bought one of Herr Baedeker's pocket-size guidebooks. Thanks to its amazing store of details, she managed to lead us through Belgard as if she had been born there.

The city was graciously and beautifully laid out, with broad avenues and unexpected, though somewhat neglected, little garden spots. The gilded cupolas of the Albertine Palace lay on one side of the river, the spacious Ritterhof Square on the other. Though a number of coffeehouses and restaurants had gone out of business, their windows empty or boarded up, the remaining establishments did offer open terraces, usually with an old fellow plunking a zither, or a fiddler scraping out waltzes.

Vendors hawked miniature flags, and what shops were open had bravely bedecked themselves with banners. The ever-present chicken paprika had been renamed Chicken Maria-Sophia. The passersby bustled about good-naturedly as if they were all hurrying to their last party and had made up their minds to forget their troubles and enjoy it.

For the fact was, as Vesper quickly observed, a threadbare atmosphere lay just below the colorful surface. The frequent groups of men and women drifting along the streets were not pleasure-seekers; they were out of work. Street musicians played for pennies and collected very few of those small coins. And, alas, Belgard had more than its share of beggars, among them not a few children.

Another difficulty threatened to mar the jubilee: the growing ill will between Drackenberg and the Kingdom of Carpatia. The latter had been drumming up a movement to annex the grand duchy and, in effect, turn it into a Carpatian province. Even some of the Drackenberg population claimed annexation would bring much-needed prosperity. Indeed, Belgard's biggest newspaper featured noisy articles which, in a less easygoing country, would have put the editor in the dock for high treason. Most, however, adored Maria-Sophia and shrugged off the views of their opponents. As a local saying went: "Two Dracken-bergers, five and a half opinions."

Vesper, who never has difficulty forming her own opinions, insisted on wearing the red-and-black rosette of the anti-annexation party. As Philadelphians, Mary and I naturally favored independence. Nevertheless, I reminded Vesper that local squabbles did not concern us; we were merely sightseers. As planned, we would attend the grand ball in the Albertine Palace at the end of the week, ob-serve the public ceremonies, then return home. I urged her to make the most of our brief holiday.

"Then we shouldn't miss Schwanfeld Castle." Vesper consulted her Baedeker. "Built by the present Count Wil-helm Karolyi-Walsegg as his country retreat, a striking example of architectural fantasy. Unique collection of curi-ous objets d'art and antiquities, fifteenth-century painting, thirty-six rooms exotically decorated. And so on. It sounds worth seeing."

Very likely it was. But, as I pointed out, Schwanfeld Castle was evidently a private residence. Count Wilhelm could hardly be expected to welcome strangers.

"I think he'd be delighted to show off his castle," said Vesper, "after he went to the trouble of building it. I'm sure he won't turn us away. I'll see to that."

I had no doubt she would.

Accordingly, that morning, I hired an open carriage and a driver who knew the roads. For the occasion, Ves-per and Mary wore tasteful travel costumes from Mr. Wanamaker's Philadelphia emporium. It was a pleasure to relax in the carefree company of the two persons dearest in the world to me. For all her rather high-handed way of going about it, Vesper had been quite right in wanting us to visit Drackenberg. Our excursion to the castle could well prove to be one of our happiest outings.

We reached Schwanfeld by early afternoon, rolling past golden meadows and handsome stretches of woodland. Red-and-white cows grazed in the pastures of Hänsel-and-Gretel cottages, with the highest peaks of the Carlomanians just visible in the distance. Vesper was delighted—and puzzled.

"You'd think there'd be visitors by the dozens touring a country with a landscape like this," she exclaimed. "But except for us, I haven't seen a single carriage on the roads."

That, I replied, was a blessing.

"Not for Drackenberg," said Vesper. "It needs money, doesn't it? If people found out what they were missing, they'd flock here, it seems to me. And the money they'd spend would help a lot."

Our driver turned off the road and followed a fairly smooth forest track, emerging at a clearing that gave us our first sight of the castle. At this, Vesper continued her remarks about tourists—or the lack of them.

"Doesn't anybody outside Drackenberg know about this? Schwanfeld alone—that's enough to bring visitors from around the world." Vesper stood up in the carriage for a better view. "Architectural fantasy? It's a fairy tale! It belongs under a Christmas tree!"

Mary was equally enchanted. I had seen larger structures in the valleys of the Rhine and the Loire, but none of such flamboyant eccentricity. What it lacked in size

Schwanfeld made up in variety. One tower was capped by a gracefully sloping roof; another looked like an Arabian Nights minaret; still another displayed a Gothic belfry with attendant gargoyles.

A moat, overgrown with duckweed, circled the ivied walls. The drawbridge had been lowered, allowing us to clatter across it into a cobbled courtyard.

"You can see that it used to be a fortress," said Vesper, "but obviously Count Wilhelm's rebuilt it every which way."

Springing from the carriage, she called Mary's attention to a garden ringed with topiary hedges trimmed into the shape of swans, lions, and elephants. While they marveled at this green menagerie, I approached the main building. The massive iron door knocker was wrought in the form of a satyr's goat-horned head. As I raised it, a tongue impudently popped out of the creature's mouth.

Eventually, the door opened. An ancient fellow in rusty black livery peered at me. I presented my card and asked if we might have the honor of speaking with Count Wilhelm. We had come from Philadelphia to attend the jubilee and had journeyed to Schwanfeld for the purpose of admiring the castle.

He stared at me as if he had never heard of Philadelphia. Shaking his head, he launched into what I took to be the local dialect, a mixture of German going in one direction and Hungarian in another. I gathered only that it was impossible for His Excellency to see us.

Vesper and Mary had joined me during this exchange. With her fluency in languages, Vesper was able to comprehend him better than I.

"Baedeker's a little out of date," she told me. "Count Wilhelm certainly can't see us. He died last year. His son, Count Sigismund, is the heir. But we can't see him either. He's not in residence."

In that case, I replied, we had made a long excursion for nothing.

"Of course not," said Vesper. "Mr. Pognor here will be glad to show us around. That's what he was trying to tell you."

The aged caretaker beckoned us to enter. Already taken aback by the impudent door knocker, I was prepared to expect anything.

Or so I thought.

CHAPTER

≈ 2 ≈

Even the most seasoned traveler, who has observed bi-
zarre scenes and situations throughout much of the world,
would not expect to come face to face, for example, with
a giant plaster troll. Yet this was the first object we encountered on entering the grand hall.

"*Wasser,*" declared Pognor. "*Wasser! Achtung!*"

The fellow must have activated a mechanism of some
sort, for the monstrous troll suddenly sprayed a jet of
water from its nose, nearly drenching me.

"I see what Baedeker means by 'curious,' " Vesper remarked.

Mary actually giggled. I found nothing humorous in
such a welcome and so stated. Pognor, clearly much taken
by Vesper, bobbed his head and beamed at her, beckon-
ing the *gnädiges Fräulein* to accompany him.

"He's really delighted to see us," Vesper said. "The
other servants are gone. If I understand him, he's hardly
spoken to anyone for months."

The aged caretaker ushered us through room after room filled with a hodgepodge of antique weapons, Greek statues, Hindu figures, and artificial birds that twittered and flapped their wings. Vesper and Mary would gladly have lingered, but I was in no frame of mind to appreciate the late Count Wilhelm's eccentricities.

Pognor eventually led us into the gallery housing the collection of fifteenth-century paintings, undeniably excellent and impressive: a magnificent Botticelli, a Verrocchio, a couple of battle scenes by Uccello, and other splendid works set higgledy-piggledy among lesser and unknown artists.

I would have lagged behind to examine the Botticelli, but I heard Mary gasp in astonishment.

"Look at this portrait," she urged as I hurried to join her. "Brinnie—it could be Vesper herself. Her sister, in any case."

To me, the portrait merely showed a plainly costumed young woman gazing directly at the viewer. The artist had depicted her seated, surrounded by books, manuscripts, a set of lenses, chemical or alchemical apparatus, a lute, and other assorted musical instruments.

True, the young woman had long and beautiful tresses. But, I pointed out, they were light brown, not marmalade; the eyes were hazel, not Vesper's startling green.

"My dear Brinnie, ever literal-minded," said Mary. "Those are details. I refer to the spirit, the personality."

I studied the portrait again. After several moments, I understood something of what Mary had so quickly seen: the same bold glance, the same air of luminous intelligence, and a very similar expression around the mouth, half-curved in a quizzical smile. Yes, there was a definitely Vesperish quality.

The dear girl herself seemed not especially aware of the resemblance. This was only natural. How many of us see ourselves as others do? Nevertheless, she did sense an affinity.

"I like her," Vesper said. "I wish I could have met her. We'd have been friends."

Pognor, hovering behind us, must have noticed the likeness, too. He babbled away excitedly, pointing first to Vesper and then the portrait.

"Gnädiges Fräulein! Gräfin von Italien! Two beauties, *ja?"*

Vesper spoke with him briefly and turned back to us.

"She's the Countess Cecilia. Pognor doesn't know much about her. They've always called her the *Gräfin von Italien.* She married into the Karolyi family long before they connected with the Walseggs.

"What's interesting," Vesper went on, "is that there's another picture of her. No, not in the gallery," she added as I glanced around. "Here in the painting."

My attention had gone more to the features of the countess than to the objects beside her. One of them, as Vesper indicated, was indeed another portrait partly concealed by drapery.

Vesper, of course, was familiar with this artistic device: the painter's way, no doubt, of showing off his cleverness at duplicating a fellow artist's work. Della Croce, in his picture of Mozart, had shown a detailed portrait of the young composer's mother. Courbet, that scandalous Frenchman, showed himself at work on his own canvas.

Philadelphia's illustrious Charles Willson Peale included some antique busts in his family scene. In the case of Countess Cecilia, it was a smaller portrait, only the head and shoulders, but painstakingly rendered as what must have been an exact copy.

"The funny thing is," Vesper said, "the portrait in the painting is better than the portrait on the wall."

Vesper has the eye of an art connoisseur or a horse trader. Never would I dream of questioning her judgment in either of those delicate areas. She was, of course, correct. Even I could detect the excellence suggested by the duplicate.

"If the copy's that good," said Vesper, "the original must be still better, the best one in the whole collection. A lot better than some of those ancestral portraits. Some of the old Karolyis look like they have indigestion. I wonder what they thought of Countess Cecilia. I'd bet they didn't get along too well."

Vesper, I am convinced, is unique. Just as well, too. The world could not accommodate more than one of her at a time. Had Countess Cecilia's personality resembled Vesper's to any degree, I could imagine her making quite a stir among the solemn Karolyis.

"I wish I could have a look at that picture," Vesper went on. "Pognor says it isn't here. He has no idea where it is. He's never seen it since he's been at Schwanfeld."

We left the portrait, then, and strolled through the rest of the gallery. Vesper wished to tour the remainder of the castle. So did my dear Mary, who showed no sign at all of fatigue despite our fairly long and strenuous excursion. But I had to insist on leaving immediately if we wanted to reach Belgard before dark.

They reluctantly agreed and I was finally able to tear them away from Schwanfeld, leaving Pognor bowing happily to Vesper and making hand-kissing gestures.

"We'll come back another time," Vesper declared, as we headed back toward the city. "After the grand ball.

"Doesn't it strike you as odd," she went on, while our carriage clattered through the gathering dusk, "that the portrait should be missing? Cecilia would have taken good care of it, I'm sure. You can tell that right away from all the other things in the picture.

"Think about it, Brinnie. Her lute, her books, all the rest—I'd guess they were what she treasured most. Why else would she want them in the picture? I can understand that. If somebody painted my portrait, I'd want Moggie with me, and my banjo, my telescope—"

I broke in to say that I grasped the point.

"All right," Vesper went on, "if she treasured those other things, she treasured the portrait, too."

Perhaps, perhaps not. It was customary, I replied, for painters to include such items to show their subject's prosperity, for the sake of impressing the beholder. Fifteenth-century nobility enjoyed flaunting their jewels, clothing, and all such possessions.

"Not Cecilia," said Vesper, as if she had known the young countess all her life. "She wouldn't care about impressing anyone. No, those things meant something personal to her."

"That's as may be," I answered. "It makes no difference now. She's gone, and so is the portrait. If Pognor knows nothing of it, no one does."

"What a shame," said Vesper. "It was her favorite, I'll

bet it was. How do you guess she'd feel, knowing it had vanished? She wouldn't like it. Neither would I."

My heart sank for an instant. I expected the dear girl to take it on herself to find the painting. She had led us on equally wild goose chases. However, she said no more and settled back in the carriage. I heaved a sigh of relief.

"Brinnie, we'll try to find that painting," she said a moment later. "What's the trouble? Swallow wrong? We should look for it, anyway. Pognor told me we can rummage around all we want. Why not? It's the least we can do for Cecilia."

CHAPTER

3

When Vesper seizes on an idea she considers a good one, it is difficult to get the dear girl unclenched from it. Ordinarily, she sets her projects in train without delay. This time, she did not.

There were two reasons.

First, as we continued on our way, Mary drowsed with her head on my shoulder, and I took the opportunity to speak calmly and reasonably with Vesper. I explained, with clearest logic, why such a quest would prove fruitless. Vesper stayed silent, which is not always a good sign. Nevertheless, by the time we reached Belgard I was satisfied I had convinced her.

Second, she had other, and more urgent, things to do. The grand reception was to be held the next evening. The flurry of last-minute preparations drove any further thoughts about Countess Cecilia from her mind. Mary and Vesper had odds and ends of shopping to finish. I would have gone along to keep a protective eye on them, but Mary declined my offer.

"You'll make a nuisance of yourself, Brinnie," Mary told me. "We don't want you underfoot."

I had the impression they preferred being on their own. Since Vesper assured me they would return in time for lunch, I felt confident they would encounter no difficulties in that short space of time. I settled down with some English newspapers, but close to noon, a commotion from Ritterhof Square drew my attention.

I went out onto the balcony. The square was taking on an increasingly festive look. The stands and platform had been completed; work crews had nailed up bunting, festooning the railway terminal and raising a sort of triumphal arch near the bridge spanning the River Presta.

I could distinguish little more than a swirling tussle of figures: a crowd hastily gathering, with some of the onlookers joining the fray. Within moments, a squad of Belgard constables arrived at a run and, soon after, a horse-drawn police van. The officers briskly set about dispersing the idlers and hustling the more obstreperous into the vehicle.

Had it not surpassed belief, I would have sworn I recognized Mary's slender figure. Then, to my consternation, I glimpsed a flash of unmistakably marmalade-colored hair.

Shouting, from this height and distance, was useless. I did so anyway. Then, still in my dressing gown, I dashed from the balcony, out of our suite, and raced down several flights of stairs.

By the time I reached the street, the incident, whatever it had been, was over; the crowd scattered, the van carrying off my loved ones out of sight.

There was not a cab to be found. Despite my state of undress, I was prepared to follow the police van on foot. Then I caught sight of a man in a smock, his white hair straggling from under a floppy beret.

I recognized him as the photographer from the studio next to the bookshop. He had just finished loading a tripod onto a cart filled with other equipment of his profession. I hurried to him.

"I beg you, for heaven's sake," I cried out, "transport me to the police station—*Polizeiwache,* whatever it is called here."

He looked me up and down as if that was where I belonged. Finally, he shrugged and gestured for me to climb aboard. The horse clopped along at an infuriatingly slow pace. At last, my driver pointed out the building I required. I hardly thanked the good fellow as I jumped down and ran through the main receiving area, shaking off any constables who tried to hinder me.

In one of the larger offices, I sighted Mary and Vesper seated across the table from a gray-haired man of obviously high rank.

Vesper and I have had our share of brushes with the law. The dear girl, I knew, was quite capable of dealing with them. But the sight of my gentle, innocent Mary in the brutal clutches of some foreign official was more than I could bear. I flung myself into the office.

"My dear sir," I burst out, making no attempt to conceal my indignation, "this is nothing less than outrageous! Surely these ladies have told you they are Philadelphians, guests in your city at the personal invitation of Her Highness. I demand their immediate release."

21

Mary, I feared, was too terrified and humiliated to express a word of relief at my timely arrival; then I realized she had just taken a large mouthful of Drackenbergertorte. Vesper observed my dishevelment with curiosity.

"What have you been up to, Brinnie?" she calmly inquired. "You'd better have a cup of coffee."

The official, identifying himself as Inspector Lenz, rose and gave me an elegant bow.

"Sir," he said, with a bemused glance, "it is not possible for me to release them."

"Then, sir," I cried, "you shall have me to deal with!"

"Herr Professor Garrett, as I presume you are," he replied, "you misunderstand. I cannot release them for the excellent reason that they are not under arrest. They were brought here for their own protection as well as that of others involved in this unhappy affair. They could have suffered serious injury."

"Not us," Vesper put in. "He means the ones who started it."

"We were accosted," said Mary. "I do not tolerate being accosted under any circumstances, neither in Philadelphia nor anywhere else. I simply will not stand for it."

"Aunt Mary used a handbag on them," said Vesper.

"It was, I am told, a heavy handbag," added Lenz. "Given the manner in which the Frau Professor wielded it, I might classify it as a lethal weapon."

"We were coming back to the hotel," Vesper said, aware of my growing bewilderment, "when that bunch of baboons saw my rosette."

"They were highly provocative, Brinnie," put in Mary.

"The fact that they do not agree with the dear child's views cannot excuse their behavior."

"This is not the first such incident," said Lenz. "We have had, regrettably, a number of more serious altercations with those who favor annexation by Carpatia. We have, in fact, strong suspicions that bands of brawlers have been paid to create disturbances. Even so, as a police officer, my duty is to keep the peace impartially. But, if I may speak in a personal capacity, I shall not be sorry to see these troublemakers under lock and key. As they will be."

He motioned with his head, and I watched a gang of some half-dozen ruffians being led away to the cells.

"I cannot detain them as long as I would wish," said Lenz. "But I assure you they will not press charges against your wife."

"What?" I exclaimed. "What charges?"

"There might have been a nose damaged," put in Vesper.

"Two," Mary corrected, "possibly a third. It was, as this kind Mr. Lenz told you, a very heavy bag."

"We are not keeping count of noses," said Lenz. "I suggest we call the incident happily closed."

That I was glad to do. I was still trying to digest the idea of my gentle, mild-tempered Mary devastating that band of ruffians. Lenz shook hands with all of us and went with us to the door.

"You are attending the reception, are you not?" he said. "To make up for any distress to the charming Fräulein Holly and the Frau Professor, allow me the honor of providing you with an escort to the palace."

"Sir, I was not in any way distressed," said Mary.

23

"Of course you weren't," said Vesper. "But if Inspector Lenz offers an escort, we can't refuse."

"You are right, dear child." Mary smiled graciously. "Yes, I think I'd enjoy that."

Inspector Lenz was good as his word and better. That night, by the time we were ready to leave, we were greeted at our carriage by a troop of mounted gendarmes very handsomely turned out and, as well, a company of Belgard firemen in bright uniforms and polished helmets. They conducted us across the bridge, through the gate, and to the very steps of the Albertine Palace.

I can only say that we arrived there in greater style than any of the other guests, whatever their rank. In Philadelphia, this might have been considered a shade ostentatious. Still, Vesper and Mary deserved no less.

They were, beyond question, the belles of the ball. The grand hall was already crowded when we entered, the room ablaze with candles, the high, vaulted ceilings reflecting a golden glitter. There were liveried footmen everywhere, in old-style costumes and powdered wigs of a century ago, and cuirassiers in plumed helmets and shining breastplates, almost as impressive as our own First City Troop. An orchestra played from an upper gallery. I observed what I assumed to be royals: the men with blue sashes across their white shirtfronts, the ladies with tiaras or coronets. Vesper cast an appraising eye around her.

"They've spent a fortune on this party," she remarked. "I don't begrudge Her Highness having a celebration. But if the rest of the country's badly off, I don't call it fair."

Maria-Sophia, I pointed out, was probably straining her own personal finances for the sake of appearances. In principle, of course, Vesper was right. And yet, I could not help being gratified by the presence of my two dear stars, for Vesper and Mary outsparkled every other guest.

As for Vesper, on our other journeys I had been used to seeing her in tatters instead of a ball gown. Here, she was magnificent, her unbound tresses more dazzling in their natural beauty than any crown or coronet. Her costume of white satin enhanced her usual gracefulness as she moved—nay, floated—through the assemblage, turning heads wherever she passed, a noble and true daughter of Philadelphia.

"When do we eat?" said Vesper, glimpsing the buffet in an adjoining hall. "Since they've put out so much food, at least we shouldn't let it go to waste."

Court custom, I reminded her, forbade refreshment until the appearance of the grand duchess.

"Where is she, then?" said Vesper. "She's late for her own party."

I explained that a reigning monarch traditionally arrived last. Vesper accepted this with fortitude, though glancing from time to time at the buffet. Mary had been captured by a circle of admirers; I lost track of her in the crowd and would have set about looking for her, but Vesper suddenly held me back.

"Over there, Brinnie," she murmured, "talking to that weedy fellow with the blue sash."

At first, I could not see to whom she referred. Then the breath went out of me.

In cheerful conversation with one of the royals—a fop-

pish figure with a pencil-line mustache and an abundance of macassar oil on his dark ringlets—stood the vilest of all creatures.

It was Dr. Desmond Helvitius.

I could only stare dumbstruck at this scoundrel with his deeply tanned features and great shock of white hair. On a scarlet ribbon at his throat glittered the jeweled star of some sort of honorable order. His impeccably tailored evening coat bore other medals and decorations—all of them surely as false as their wearer.

Dr. Helvitius caught sight of Vesper at the same time. He covered his astonishment with a smile, disengaged himself from his partner in conversation, and had the effrontery to make his way toward us.

Murderous villain that he was, I would have turned my back on him. Vesper, however, looked squarely at him. Whatever emotions the dear girl felt at confronting this fiend who had so often sought to destroy us, her features remained calm.

"My pleasure, dear Miss Holly and Professor Garrett, is equaled only by my surprise." Dr. Helvitius bowed ceremoniously. "While I hoped our previous meeting would not be our final one, I confess I did not expect that hope to be so quickly fulfilled."

I could not say likewise. Our last encounter with Helvitius had been during an earthquake. From the deck of his yacht on the Rio Culebra, the wretch had been directing rapid fire upon us by means of a Gatling gun. Uncharitable it may be, but I fervently wished he had found a permanent place under the debris of the horrendous mud slide that grounded his vessel and allowed us barely to escape with our lives.

Vesper smiled at him. "That was really a piece of bad luck in El Dorado."

"Bad luck?" replied Helvitius. "As you see, I emerged from the jungle with a minimum of inconvenience."

"That's what I meant," said Vesper.

Helvitius gave a cheery grin full of teeth. He gestured expansively around the ballroom. "Here, beneath this golden dome we meet, as it were, under a flag of truce. I am in no frame of mind for petty squabbling. On this festive occasion, our common purpose is to honor Her Highness and to enjoy the evening, as I intend to do.

"I say only this to you," he added. "Meddle in my affairs here and I shall see that you live precisely long enough to regret it.

"Now, Miss Holly, will you promise me the first waltz?"

CHAPTER

4

"I will and I won't," said Vesper. "I won't promise you the waltz. That belongs to Brinnie. Your affairs? I don't know what they are, but I mean to find out. When I do, I'll meddle in them. I promise you that."

"Then, Miss Holly," replied Helvitius, never dropping his air of conviviality, "and you, Professor Garrett: Your lives, as of this moment, are as good as lost."

Vesper stayed unruffled. Helvitius might as well have offered nothing more threatening than a comment on the weather. For me, the encounter had taken on the quality of some grotesque dream: the two of them chatting in the midst of this dazzling assemblage, the orchestra playing snatches of Offenbach, the elegantly garbed Helvitius pleasantly vowing to exterminate us. It was more unsettling than his blazing away at us with a Gatling gun or heaving sticks of dynamite. In such situations, things are open and aboveboard. One knows what one has to deal with.

His threat had to be taken seriously, but it was all the more aggravating coming from such a reprehensible individual, and one of such arrogance. Apart from his enormous wealth, he looked on himself as a scholar and connoisseur, outrageously proud of his achievements in chemistry, mineralogy, and archeology. I would not have been surprised if the wretch even had literary pretensions.

A royal reception is no proper setting for any but the most trivial social exchanges; yet I was close to expressing some harsh opinions directly to his face. Before I could do so, Helvitius gave us a suddenly baleful glance and turned on his heel to mingle with the crowd.

"Dear girl," I whispered, "we must leave here instantly."

Vesper stood silent and thoughtful. At that moment, Mary rejoined us.

"What a splendid gathering, Brinnie," she said. "Who was that distinguished-looking gentleman speaking with you?"

Vesper did not answer, nor did I. Seeing Mary's smiling face, how could we tell her then and there that he was no gentleman and was distinguished only by ruthless cruelty? I cast about for some way to reveal, without dampening her spirits, that he had just vowed to do away with us.

Fortunately, for the time being, we were spared that unhappy task. The orchestra now struck up the Drackenberg national anthem.

The crowd parted to make way for the Grand Duchess Maria-Sophia as she progressed toward a draped platform at the far end of the ballroom—or rather, as she stumped ahead briskly, aided by a knobby cane more an Irish shillelagh than a royal walking stick. Though one of the most elderly rulers in Europe, she had a jaw that looked strong enough to crack walnuts and a pair of sharp, shrewd blue eyes as hard edged as the diamonds in her crown.

"She looks like the Drackenberg flag," said Vesper.

The emblem of the grand duchy is a golden dragon, and Vesper detected the resemblance precisely. Maria-Sophia had ties with every royal line and it showed in her features: the full Hapsburg lip, the hawkish Bourbon nose. There were still hints of the russet hair of the Elphbergs in her gray tresses. This combination, plus a beetling brow and a crackling glance, gave a definitely dragonlike air. It would be prudent to keep a safe distance from her.

"I want to talk to her," said Vesper. "We have to tell her about Helvitius."

"And if she already knows?" I countered.

"I'll find that out," said Vesper.

I doubted she would have the opportunity. Her Highness had no sooner taken her seat than attendants began herding the guests into line and hustling them past Maria-Sophia as rapidly as they could.

When our turn came, Mary had time only for a brief curtsy before a gentleman usher moved her promptly along. Vesper, however, planted her feet and ignored the attendant's frowns and gestures.

"Your Highness," Vesper said, "do you realize one of your guests is a murderous criminal?"

The face of the grand duchess held a fixed smile, the sort of expression royals learn from the cradle and use during public functions. She ignored Vesper's declaration entirely.

"Your Highness—" Vesper began again.

By this time, a gentleman-in-waiting had taken Vesper firmly by the elbow. She tried to turn back, but attendants to monarchs are good at their work. Vesper, I think, was surprised at how efficiently she was whisked down the steps, while I was allowed less than a moment for the hastiest of bows.

"Didn't she understand me?" Vesper muttered indignantly. "Was she even listening? All right, Brinnie, I'll find some way to get her attention."

"Dear girl," I replied, "forget about the grand duchess. We must leave without another moment's delay." Belgard, I knew, had one outbound train, departing for Carpatia at noon. We had time to pack, vacate the hotel suite, and be well away from Drackenberg and Helvitius.

"Not on your life," said Vesper. "Mine either."

With Helvitius, I pointed out, it might well come to that.

"Before we decide anything, I want a few more words with Maria-Sophia," Vesper said. "No point running away unless we have to. It would be a shame to spoil Aunt Mary's holiday."

Sudden death, I remarked, could mar the happiest occasion.

"Whatever Helvitius is up to," said Vesper, "I'm not leaving Drackenberg until I put a couple of spokes in his wheel. Once I make Maria-Sophia understand, she'll have to do something about him."

Mary, fortunately, was not present to hear our conversation. The refreshment room was now open, and she had been swept into it by the tide of other guests. For Vesper,

31

the buffet had lost its attraction. She hung back, highly unsatisfied by Maria-Sophia's lack of concern.

I explained to Vesper that she could expect no further audience. Now that the procession of guests had ended, the grand duchess would withdraw into some private dining room. We had, in effect, seen the last of her.

"I haven't," said Vesper.

The dear girl, surely, would have tracked the dragon to its very lair. To my relief, this was not necessary. One of the ushers now approached and, surprisingly, announced that Her Highness desired our presence.

"I'll bet she does," remarked Vesper.

I followed her as she strode back to the platform, where Maria-Sophia had remained.

Her Highness no longer had her previous glazed expression. On the contrary, she fixed a penetrating and rather daunting glance on Vesper.

"Young woman, if that was your idea of a joke, I was not amused."

"Neither was I," returned Vesper. "Your Highness—"

"The only reason I arranged to see you again," Maria-Sophia went on, "is that I have been informed of your connection with a diplomatic official whom I respected. Now, then, what the devil do you mean? You tell me I am entertaining a criminal? I am not responsible for all the unlikely individuals at my reception—you, for example, Miss Holly."

"Well, if you'd give me a chance to explain," began Vesper.

"That," said Maria-Sophia, "is what I am doing."

Her Highness snapped her jaw shut and stayed silent

32

while Vesper offered the essential facts regarding Helvitius.

"Bombs? Gatling guns? Trying to bury you alive?" Her Highness snorted. "You Americans, I understand, are given to tall tales. Very well, there is one way to settle this."

Maria-Sophia then ordered Helvitius summoned to her. But there was no sign of him. Her Highness shrugged and gave Vesper a skeptical look.

"He must have left as soon as we finished talking," Vesper insisted. "Before that, I saw him with a ferrety sort of fellow with a blue sash and a lot of hair oil. A sneaky little mustache—"

"That," Maria-Sophia said icily, "happens to be Count Bertrand, my grandnephew."

"Send for him," said Vesper. "Ask him yourself."

"Do you presume to give me orders?" Her Highness shot Vesper a glare that would have sent an ordinary mortal running for cover. Vesper, however, stood her ground. Her Highness studied her with a cold, appraising glance for several moments, then dispatched an attendant to fetch the young nobleman.

There was no sign of him, either. Count Bertrand had vanished as completely as Helvitius.

Although Vesper insisted that she had seen the two of them together with her own eyes, Maria-Sophia looked as if smoke and flames might stream from her nostrils.

"Young woman, until you have evidence to substantiate your accusations, you will desist from making them." Her Highness turned a baleful eye on me. "As for you, I might overlook the adolescent fantasies of your ward, but you should have better sense than to permit her to indulge them. You may consider this audience terminated. You may also take your leave."

Vesper was fuming when we left Her Highness and went to find Mary in the refreshment room.

"Adolescent fantasies, are they?" she muttered. "That little weasel is up to something with Helvitius. I'd like to get my hands on him."

Still a bit shaken by our audience, and grateful that Her Highness had only whacked the floor instead of our heads, I strongly insisted on returning immediately to our hotel to decide our next step. The first train out of Belgard was the obvious choice.

Mary, enjoying herself at the buffet, was much put out when I announced that we must leave the reception. So, too, was Vesper. For the sake of their safety, I paid no heed to their protests and led them from the palace to our waiting carriage. The escort which Lenz had provided was still on hand and I was grateful for it. As we rode across the bridge, I decided that it was best to come straight out and tell Mary, as delicately as possible, that our lives were in danger and, very briefly, mention our previous experiences with that vile scoundrel Helvitius.

"I am distressed to hear that, Brinnie," Mary replied. "Had I thought you would lead the dear child into such circumstances with such undesirable individuals, I would have insisted on going with you. It pains me to say it, my dear Brinnie, but sometimes I wonder if you are to be entirely trusted by yourself."

There was no use in explaining that earthquakes and volcanic eruptions were none of my doing. I was relieved to have reached our hotel safely. We passed the concierge, snoring at his desk in the lobby, and made our way upstairs to our suite. With a sigh of relief, I double-bolted the door behind us.

"What a lovely and thoughtful gift," exclaimed Mary, pointing to a large basket on the table.

It was, indeed, a luxurious assortment of Drackenberg sausages, wedges of cheese, and a cold roast chicken.

"That's nice." Vesper brightened a little. "The concierge must have brought it while we were out."

"Who could have sent it?" said Mary. "Perhaps that charming Inspector Lenz?"

I went to see if a card was attached. Vesper followed me. Having missed the buffet, the dear girl was no doubt eager to sample these delicacies.

"Brinnie, stay back," she suddenly ordered. "Sausages don't tick."

5

The dear girl has ears sharper than any human being I have met. Certainly, I myself was unaware of any ticking sausages and, in fact, was about to examine the generous gift when Vesper darted past me. She snatched up the basket and heaved it with all her might at the casement window.

It was almost too late. That same instant, I did hear the click of some sort of mechanism and, in horror, understood the diabolical nature of the seemingly innocent Drackenbergerwurst. I barely had time to fling my bewildered Mary to the floor. Even as it shattered the window, the basket exploded.

The blast rocked our sitting room and carried away a portion of the balcony. A cloud of acrid smoke filled the air. Once sure my dear Mary was unharmed, I scrambled to my feet and called out to Vesper. The dear girl had been quick witted and nimble footed enough to take shelter behind a divan. I gave a cry of relief and ran to her side.

"You'd better sit down, Brinnie," said Vesper, dusting herself off. "You look as if you've had a nasty shock."

My gentle Mary is unaccustomed to violent episodes; yet, to my astonishment, she displayed a calmness and presence of mind equal to Vesper's. That is to say, she was more indignant than terrified.

"You could have had us all blown up, Brinnie, if the dear child had not kept her wits about her." She went to put her arms around Vesper. "Are you quite all right, child? Your gown, I fear, is ruined."

Unharmed though we were, all of us presented a distressing appearance, dusted with plaster and smudged with black smoke that still hung in the room. I followed Vesper's advice and, head reeling, sank down on the remains of the divan.

"Helvitius meant what he said," remarked Vesper. "He didn't wait for us to meddle in his affairs."

By this time, the concierge had come bursting through the door, which hung askew on its hinges. Whether or not he understood we had barely escaped with our lives, he was furious at the damage to the hotel suite. The blast had also drawn the attention of our escort, which had not yet passed beyond Ritterhof Square. In the street below, the fire brigade rang alarm bells, which only added to the commotion in our room. Half a dozen gendarmes arrived on the heels of the concierge, who was waving his arms and accusing us of being disorderly guests.

The aftereffects of the explosion having left me somewhat muddled, I was not in a frame of mind to pay much heed to the concierge. One of the gendarmes must have sent for Inspector Lenz. Within what seemed to me, in my confused state, a short period of time, that excellent official arrived in our suite. Somewhat disheveled, no doubt roused from his bed, Inspector Lenz put some order into the situation by force of his authoritative presence.

"All he can find out right now," Vesper told me, "is that the concierge let a man take a basket of food up to our rooms. And we're being requested to vacate the premises—as if we were the ones to blame."

"This is altogether deplorable," added Lenz, who now came to join us. "The explosive device, one of my officers tells me, was a very simple detonating mechanism run by clockwork. It could have been assembled quickly and easily."

"Yes," I burst out angrily, "by the vile hand of Helvitius himself."

"He had plenty of time to do it after he disappeared from the reception," Vesper said. "He wouldn't have had much trouble to find out where we were staying."

"And you can certainly stay here no longer," put in Lenz. "The device would have exploded whether you were in the room or not. So, I cannot say if it was designed to frighten you or destroy you. Either way, it would have suited the purposes of your enemy. You can be sure he will strike again."

His words convinced me all the more that we must take the first train out of Belgard.

"What do we do meantime?" replied Vesper. "We can't sit around and wait for Helvitius to blast us again."

"I can offer you the protection of one of our cells," Lenz told her. "Poor hospitality, but altogether safe."

"You propose to put us in jail?" inquired Mary. "Yes,

that would be a novel experience. I assume we would have private accommodations?"

"Before we decide about the inspector's jail," put in Vesper, "I'm going to the palace. Maria-Sophia wanted evidence? She'll have it now."

Despite my protests that Her Highness would not receive us at this time of night, if ever, Vesper was determined to go back to the Albertine.

"Then, Miss Holly," said Lenz, "allow me to assist you. Her Highness and I are old friends. I can gain admission for you in my personal, as well as my official, capacity. If you wish, I shall take you there in my own carriage."

"Good," said Vesper. "We'll do it right now." Mary wished to change into less bedraggled costume, but Vesper refused. "No, Aunt Mary, we'll go exactly as we are. I want Maria-Sophia to see for herself. If I'm going to tell her about an explosion, I want to show her we've been through one."

The grand reception was still in progress when Inspector Lenz drove us to the palace. Her Highness, though, had retired, and the inspector was obliged to exert all the influence of both his personal and official capacities before we were conducted to Maria-Sophia's private apartments.

The grand duchess had replaced her formal attire with a not very elegant kimono. She was sitting on a chaise longue, soaking her feet in a basin of water.

"The Philadelphians again?" she burst out. "Gottlieb, what the devil do you mean by this?"

Vesper was in no mood to stand on ceremony. She

strode up to Maria-Sophia and, without mincing words, told what had happened to us.

"Inspector Lenz has kindly offered to lock us up in jail," Vesper concluded. "Before we go, I just wanted you to have a look at poor Brinnie and Aunt Mary. I don't think you'll call them adolescent fantasies."

Maria-Sophia turned a sharp eye on the inspector. "Is all this true? Exploding sausages? Indeed!"

Lenz confirmed the facts. Then he added: "Duchess Mitzi, I shall begin an investigation of the whole affair and try to lay hands on this Dr. Helvitius. But I cannot keep these people in jail permanently. Once out of my protection, even if they attempt to leave Belgard, they will be exposed to further danger."

Her Highness growled and grumbled to herself and looked as if she were chewing lumpy oatmeal. "Get on with your investigation, then. If my grandnephew Bibi— that is to say Count Bertrand—has anything whatever to do with this appalling business, I want to know about it, too. Little wretch," she muttered. "I wouldn't put anything past him. He was disgusting even when he was a baby, and worse now he's grown up.

"Furthermore, I don't like my guests being threatened, and I won't stand for them being killed." She turned a dragonish glance on Vesper. "You were invited here, so I suppose I'm responsible for you. Miss Holly, you are a very persistent young woman and, I suspect, a rather disruptive and impertinent one." With this, Maria-Sophia actually smiled. "I find that a point in your favor. At your age, I was equally so—and continue to be. But that's neither here nor there. At the moment, my first consideration is to preserve your life.

"There is only one place safer than Gottlieb's jail," added Maria-Sophia. "My palace. Until this matter is cleared up, you'll stay here. Does that meet with your approval? Or do you have any further complaints to offer?"

Vesper grinned at her. "I can't think of any."

Within a couple of hours, we and all our luggage were installed in apartments in the Albertine's west wing.

"According to Baedeker," said Vesper, who had retrieved the indispensable guide, "the architecture's Late Baroque. If you want my opinion, the plumbing's Early Medieval. But we'll manage. Better settle in for a long stay. I don't think Lenz will have an easy time getting his hands on Helvitius."

Apart from drains gurgling as if they were being strangled to death, whistling drafts, and fireplaces belching out eye-watering smoke—hardly different from Philadelphia's better private academies—the Albertine was comfortable enough. It offered many attractions and diversions. We were left on our own to enjoy them, since Her Highness was busy giving audiences to distinguished visitors: a choir of up-country yodelers in local costume; representatives of the cheesemakers guild, who rolled in a gigantic wheel of their product; folk dancers leaping about and smacking the soles of their boots. She scarcely had time for herself, much less Philadelphians in refuge.

Even so, Mary delighted in admiring the antique furniture or rambling through the gardens. The palace kitchen fascinated her. "They have enough cooks to serve an army," she told me, "but they're very slack in their duties. Really, Brinnie, they could be much better organized."

Vesper discovered the library and brought up a subject I thought, and hoped, she had forgotten.

"I found what I wanted, and a lot more," she informed me. "Countess Cecilia. She's in one of the old history books. She was the daughter of a noble Florentine family—that's why Pognor called her the *Gräfin von Italien,* the Italian contessa. She came here to be married when she was my age. She could sing and sketch; she worked out her own theory of perspective and wrote a treatise on botany. I like her better and better."

Glad as I was that my dear ones found ways to occupy themselves, my thoughts returned to Helvitius. If that monster could conceive of an exploding sausage there was, surely, no limit to his villainy. Naturally, I felt relieved that we were beyond his reach. But, in effect, we were prisoners. Palatial prisoners, but prisoners nonetheless. And palace life can rapidly grow tedious.

One incident marred an otherwise uneventful afternoon.

Mary, as usual, had gone off somewhere. Vesper and I were passing through the grand hall en route to the west wing. A delegation from Carpatia—King Rudolf kept up the pretense of maintaining formal relations—stood waiting outside Maria-Sophia's audience chamber.

We would have passed around them, but Vesper stopped in her tracks. Chatting agreeably with a couple of the Carpatian diplomats was a weedy figure, hands in pockets, his long legs encased in a pair of narrow-fitting, checkered trousers.

Vesper stared a moment, then burst out: "The weasel!"

6

"He won't duck out on me again," Vesper muttered, striding toward Count Bertrand, who appeared equally surprised to see her. The Carpatians, just then, were ushered into the audience chamber. At the sight of Vesper bearing down on him, the count hunched up his shoulders and started to sidle away.

"Hold on there," Vesper called out. "I want to talk to you."

Bibi, cornered, looked Vesper up and down. "Have we been introduced?"

"At the reception," Vesper began, "you were with Dr. Helvitius—"

"Who?" Bibi's face went blank. "Should I know him? For that matter, should I know you?"

"We are guests of Her Highness," I put in. "We have, sir, every urgent reason to inquire about your acquaintance with that man."

Count Bibi shrugged. "Not the foggiest notion. Sorry,

dear lady. Happy to oblige you if I could, but one meets so many people at these grand affairs—"

"You tell that to Her Highness," Vesper broke in. "As soon as she's finished with the Carpatians, we'll all go in and you can explain—"

"Can't be done, Miss Holly. Later, possibly. I'm off to shoot a few snipe, or grouse, or whatever's flapping about. If I'm not back for the rest of the jubilee, give dear old Auntie Mitzi all my best."

Bibi snatched the moment to detach himself from Vesper and headed down the corridor as fast as he could go. From the expression on her face, the dear girl would have followed and seized him by the collar. I urged her to let matters be. Accusations against a royal might lead to unpleasant consequences.

"Bibi's lying," retorted Vesper. "Why?"

I suggested that Count Bertrand could, in fact, be telling the truth. It was possible, and plausible, that he had merely struck up a casual conversation with Helvitius and, as he claimed, we were all total strangers to him.

"Then," replied Vesper, "how did he know my name?"

Back in our apartments, Vesper dashed off a note asking to see Her Highness, but we heard nothing from her. The poor woman was undoubtedly too swamped with Carpatian diplomats, provincial notables, and other well-wishers to be much concerned about her grandnephew. In any case, Bibi must have gone off to decimate the snipe, for we saw no more of him.

Next evening, however, Her Highness granted us an unexpected favor by inviting us to join her for a private supper in her chambers. Mary was delighted and eager. She and Vesper put on their best attire—the best, that is, remaining undamaged by the explosion. But Maria-Sophia received us dressed in the same rather tatty kimono. Her Drackenberg shillelagh leaned against her chair, ready to hand, though Her Highness seemed in less than her usual pugnacious mood. Instead, she appeared a little preoccupied and careworn.

"Bibi's a liar, of course," she told Vesper, without preamble. "He always was. But that's no help to you. I tried to get hold of him, but he's vanished again, who knows where. He has half a dozen country estates and hunting lodges—if you can say they belong to him. He's borrowed so much money on all of them.

"Gottlieb—Inspector Lenz—has nothing to report," she added. "He hasn't learned anything about Helvitius. There's no record of his arrival, his doings, or even where he's staying. For all the police know, he doesn't exist."

"He exists, that's for sure," Vesper said. "I wish he didn't."

"Be patient a little longer," said Her Highness. "The palace can't be all that disagreeable."

"It isn't," Vesper said. "I've found out a lot of interesting things. For one, you're not a dragon."

"How dare you!" burst out Maria-Sophia. "How dare you tell me I'm not a dragon!"

"Because you aren't one," said Vesper. "I've been reading about you. Before you took the throne, people could be tossed into dungeons for no reason at all. You put a stop to that. Newspapers couldn't print anything the nobility didn't like. You changed that, too. Young men

45

can't be forced to serve in the army anymore—that was your doing. That doesn't sound much like a dragon."

Maria-Sophia said nothing for a long moment, as if deciding whether to swallow Vesper in one bite or two.

She huffed a little, scowled, grumbled to herself, and finally replied, "Yes, I did all that and more. Out of my own pocket, I put up money to build an opera house. It closed. Not enough of my people could afford a ticket. I gave them an art museum, but I can't fill it with anything to attract even a handful of sightseers. My people need more than I can give them, but the country hasn't the resources for it. Child, I've failed. Do you wonder I've turned into a bad-tempered dragon?"

"But you aren't," Vesper said. "Don't tell me your people can't see through all that growling and bluster. Your people love you. I'm sure they do."

"Yes," replied Maria-Sophia, "and some of them love me so much they can't wait for Carpatia to annex them. Well, wait till they get a taste of Cousin Rudi. He was a greedy, nasty little boy and he hasn't changed a whit—except for growing a mustache. He'll put the country back where it was when I took the throne. Oh, Cousin Rudi will make them toe the mark or lop off some heads. He enjoys that.

"Why he wants poor Drackenberg in the first place," she went on, "I can't imagine. But I don't see how I can stop him."

"You have to," said Vesper. "If King Rudolf takes over, what becomes of you, let alone your people?"

"Rudi won't even take the trouble to do me in," said Maria-Sophia. "He'll pack me into some dismal corner and claim it's a rest cure. As for my people, they'll be past my help."

"No," said Vesper. "It's very simple. All you need is a way to make Drackenberg prosperous. Then there's no reason why anybody should want to be annexed."

"Simple, is it? Simple as teaching a pig to whistle." Maria-Sophia grimaced. "Believe me, child, if I could find the means, I could do all I dreamed of doing. I'd see to it my people had everything they need."

"I'm sure you would," said Vesper. "But it seems to me you'd first want to ask them what they want."

"Ask them?" cried Maria-Sophia. "Why should I ask them? I already know. Doesn't a mother know what's best for her child? My people are my children—"

"Are they?" Vesper broke in. "Maybe what they want more than anything is to grow up."

"Nonsense," Maria-Sophia snapped. "They know I love them."

"Of course you do," said Vesper. "All the more reason to let them run their own lives. You just need to find something to get the country going. Then your people can look after themselves. If they have the freedom to do it."

"You expect me to change my whole government?" exclaimed Maria-Sophia.

"I'd expect you to do the best for your people," replied Vesper. "You said that's what you wanted."

"Child, you make my head swim," said Maria-Sophia. "I let you stay in my palace and next thing I know you're stirring up— Well, I wonder. Maybe a little stirring up is what we need. It makes me feel like a girl again."

The duchess waved away further discussion. "You've

given me something to think about. I want some time to myself to chew that over. In any case, it's not your worry. I invited you for supper, not to argue affairs of state. I've had my fill of them for the day. I want something to cheer me up—and you, too. By luck, I have a treat for us."

Maria-Sophia pounded the floor with her stick and the door of an antechamber flung open.

My first impression was that we had been invaded by the loudest and wildest possible assortment of individuals who had fallen into paint pots of every conceivable color. There were, in fact, only some eight or nine, but they gave the effect of twice that many with all the racket of jingling tambourines, fiddle music, and women swirling rainbow skirts, their beads and bracelets flashing.

"Gypsies?" Vesper clapped her hands, her delight as keen as her curiosity. "How did you find them?"

"I don't have to find them," answered the duchess. "They always find me. They stop here whenever they're passing through. They know I have a soft spot for them. In the old days, Gypsies were counted worse than common criminals, fair game for anybody who wanted to hang them, shoot them, hunt them down like vermin. I changed that, too."

"I'm glad you did," said Vesper. "How could anybody want to harm them? I think they're marvelous."

"Ask Cousin Rudi," the duchess replied. "Carpatia still has terrible laws against them. Talk about annexation? If that ever happens, a Gypsy's life won't be worth a Drackenberg penny. Rudi would like to wipe them all out."

The fiddlers, meantime, switched from the lively

48

rhythms of the czardas to the most melancholy strains, then back again so quickly that my ears could not keep pace with them.

"Zoltan," Her Highness called out, "come over here, you rascal, and meet my visitors."

She addressed this command to a stocky, barrel-chested fellow leaning against the doorjamb, his thumbs hooked into a crimson sash around his ample waist. His jacket glittered with gold buttons, and a brightly patterned scarf hung rakishly around his neck. His features were sun-blackened; grizzled lovelocks curled over half his brow. His grin showed a gold tooth brighter than his buttons as he half rolled, half swaggered up to Maria-Sophia.

"Great *rawnie,*" Zoltan declaimed, making an elaborate business of kissing her hand, "if you continue to grow more beautiful, you will break my heart."

"Save that nonsense for someone foolish enough to believe it," returned the duchess, chuckling and wheezing like a leaky bellows. She introduced us then, and Zoltan bestowed equally exaggerated kisses on the hands of Mary and Vesper.

"Zoltan's a king, you should know," said Maria-Sophia. "Or so he tells me."

"No, you misunderstand," Zoltan protested. "King? That word means nothing to us. Can a king rule the wind? For we are children of the wind, great *rawnie,* and just as free. I am the *barossan,* leader of my *kumpania,* chosen by their own will.

"Now, what is true," he went on, "is that we are descended from the great pharaohs of Egypt, the land of our birth."

"Egypt?" broke in Vesper. "I've read that your people came from India."

"Read? In a book?" Zoltan threw back his head and laughed. "You believe a book, lovely *rawnie?* You trust it more than the words of a man of flesh and blood? I, Zoltan *barossan,* lay my hand on my heart and tell you it is so.

"Or," he added, shrugging his heavy shoulders, "perhaps it is not. What difference does it make?"

"If it's a matter of your own history," replied Vesper, "you'd want to know it, wouldn't you?"

"We leave history to the *gorgios.*" Zoltan put a finger to his pursed lips. "Ah, forgive me, that is not a nice word to use in such charming company. *Gorgio*—no, I should say: to those who have the great misfortune not to be *rom.* Egypt? India? To the *rom,* it is all the same. We come and go where we please."

Vesper, as a matter of scholarly interest, might have wished to delve further into the question of Zoltan's ancestry. But the fiddlers struck up another tune, and Zoltan seized Her Highness and whirled her into a czardas until she pleaded with him to have mercy on her bunions. Next thing I knew, he was spinning around with Vesper and Mary at the same time, both of them breathless from laughter as well as exertion.

Of the rest of that evening, I recall few details, understandably in view of later events. In the course of the party, Zoltan took to calling me *lavengro,* explaining that it meant "master of words," no doubt the closest his language could come to "professor." Her Highness even allowed us to address her as "Duchess Mitzi."

There was much high-spirited, even raucous behavior—from Mary as much as anyone. We stayed up deplorably late. Vesper danced as long as the Gypsies were willing to play. When Zoltan tried to draw me into a foot-stamping, tongue-clicking round, I considered it was time to take our leave and, with effort, succeeded in persuading my dear ones to do so.

Vesper roused me late next morning. Mary had already breakfasted and gone off on her customary ramblings.

"Zoltan's *kumpania* is camped in the Albertine's deer park," Vesper told me. "They won't be there long; they're soon heading south. Zoltan said we could come to see his caravan. I'd like to, and so would Aunt Mary. We'll wait until she comes back; then we'll all go and take a look."

Mary, however, did not return as expected. Even by lunchtime, she had not appeared.

"Odd." Vesper frowned. "Aunt Mary's never this late."

I assured her that Mary was busy exploring and had simply lost track of the hour.

"I suppose." Vesper, even so, had become a bit restless.

We waited a good while longer, until Vesper's uneasiness stimulated my own anxiety. To settle the matter, I rang for a footman and instructed him to find the Frau Professor and request her to join us promptly.

Almost an hour passed, while Vesper paced the apartment. There was, at last, a knock on the door. She went to open it, and quickly returned, looking unhappily puzzled.

"They can't find Aunt Mary. There's not a sign of her anywhere."

7

"How could she get lost?" Vesper said, when I suggested that Mary had strayed into some unfamiliar area. "With all the servants wandering around, she could easily ask her way. If she's in the palace, why haven't they found her?"

Vesper's penetrating intelligence has always been able to get to the bottom of the most baffling problems, and so this time I was surprised that she had not immediately grasped what was now clear to me: While the servants had been looking for Mary in one place, she had roamed on to another. They had simply missed catching up with her.

Vesper did not accept my explanation. "I don't like this, Brinnie. Something sets my teeth on edge."

I urged her to consider the matter logically. Mary, most certainly, would not have left the palace or the grounds. Therefore, she had to be in the vicinity. It was only a question of once again searching the halls and chambers more carefully and methodically.

"Then answer me this, Brinnie: Why hasn't Aunt Mary come back on her own?"

Vesper did not wait for my reply. Indeed, I had no satisfactory one to give. The footman had remained in the doorway. Vesper strode back, ordering him to report to the Albertine's majordomo with her instructions to form two large search parties, to enlist help from the guards and attendants. The dear girl had no authority to commandeer these people, but she took it anyway, and did so with as much decisiveness as the grand duchess herself.

"And tell Her Highness right away," she added, before the footman hurried to obey her orders, "that the Frau Professor is missing, and we don't know what's happened to her. Do it now. Don't worry about interrupting any audiences with bell ringers or cheese makers."

Vesper then determined that we should also begin our own search. "We'll start here in this wing of the palace and work our way room by room."

Her plan, alas, turned out to be unnecessary.

We had just stepped out of our chambers when a captain of the household guards arrived. He reported that the sentry at the palace gate had just come off duty and had taken this first opportunity to pass along an envelope.

Addressed to Miss Vesper Holly, it had been handed to him by a passerby—the sentry could give no description—who had then disappeared into the stream of traffic.

Vesper tore open the envelope. Before she read all its contents, her eyes went to the signature.

She glanced up at me, on her face a look I could not interpret.

"From Helvitius."

"He has the unmitigated gall to correspond with us?" I exclaimed. "How does the creature even know our whereabouts?"

"It's not important how he knows. The fact is, he does. Bibi saw us here and probably told him.

"Brinnie"—her voice was steady, but something in its tone gave me a twinge of alarm—"he's kidnapped Aunt Mary.

"He warns us," Vesper went on, though my mind could hardly grasp what she was saying, "we're not to leave the palace. Make no attempt to find her. At the proper time— Proper time? What's that mean?—he'll let her go unharmed. If we don't follow his orders—"

She broke off and handed me the letter. The words swam before my eyes. Without having to read it, I already knew all that mattered. Mary's life was in his clutches.

I have always taken some satisfaction in maintaining an attitude of calm rationality in even the most desperate circumstances. Now, I must accept Vesper's account of my response to this most despicable of the villain's actions.

For the fact is that I recall little of my behavior during those first sickening moments, my sensibilities being overwhelmed by the event. That Helvitius had made attempts on Vesper's life and my own was reprehensible. That he now threatened the life of my dear Mary, innocent of the least action against him, was outrageous beyond expression.

As Vesper told me later, I referred to Helvitius in terms she had never before heard me employ. According to her, I would have gone then and there into the streets of Belgard to carry out my declared intention of turning the city upside down.

Vesper made every effort to restrain me, convinced I would have done as I proposed, useless though it might have been. It was, in fact, only the dear girl's sweet voice of reason that brought me to my senses.

"Brinnie, I'll have to hit you with something if you start dashing off in all directions. Sit. Be quiet. First I'll talk to Duchess Mitzi."

We had not long to wait, for the duchess soon arrived in our apartments. When she heard Vesper's flatly stated account, and examined the letter for herself, Duchess Mitzi's jaw set and her eyes flashed. She expressed her opinion of Helvitius in phrases possibly stronger than my own.

"He won't get away with this atrocity." Duchess Mitzi pounded her stick. "I'll have the monster tracked down, wherever he may be."

"Yes, but the trouble is, where to start?" said Vesper. "How to start? For one thing, Helvitius tells us not to try to find her. For another, we don't have the slightest clue. Aunt Mary could be somewhere in Belgard, practically under our nose. She could be anyplace in Drackenberg, or maybe out of it."

That last possibility was the most alarming. Until Vesper brought it up, I had never considered that Helvitius might well have borne Mary far from the grand duchy. Here, I confess, I gave way to despair. Conducting a search of that magnitude was beyond our capabilities.

"Inspector Lenz," I exclaimed. "Send for him. Let him give us his opinion."

"We don't need opinions," said Vesper. "We need action."

At that moment, a guard who had been leading one of

the search parties arrived with one of the kitchen maids in tow. She had been overlooked until now, for she had been napping in the pantry. The distraught girl was weeping, expecting punishment for shirking her duties.

"I don't care about your duties," cried Duchess Mitzi. "If you know something, stop that sniffling and let's hear it."

By the girl's account—as best she could give it between sobs—she had seen Mary in the kitchen that morning. Shortly before, a wagon loaded with carboys of mineral water had arrived. This was not unusual; the palace routinely accepted deliveries of Nymphenwasser, a sulfurous beverage from one of the up-country spas.

"Blast all that gabble about mineral water," Duchess Mitzi burst out. "What's that got to do with anything?"

The sight of Her Highness brandishing her formidable stick threw the girl into greater confusion. She could only stammer that one of the drivers had an urgent message for the Frau Professor and insisted on speaking with her.

"Ridiculous," I put in. "Mary has no interest in discussing mineral water."

"Brinnie," Vesper suggested, "let her go on."

The girl, however, could tell us little beyond that. She had seen the Frau Professor in company of the driver and his assistant, and she had paid no further attention.

"At least that's something to go on," said Vesper, when added questions revealed nothing more and the girl was allowed to leave. "It's clear enough. Those drivers took Aunt Mary. They must have tricked her somehow."

"Then we must lay hands on them," I cried. "The police can help us. Or, by heaven, I'll take it on myself to find that villain's hirelings!"

"How?" countered Vesper. "They're hours ahead of us. Besides, if Helvitius gets wind that the police are after him—no telling what he might do. Keep Lenz out of this. For the time being, anyway."

"Then we have no help at all," I exclaimed. "Dear girl, what do you propose? I will not leave Mary a helpless victim."

"What we'll do," replied Vesper, "is exactly what Helvitius ordered."

8

"No!" I cried. "Obey that monster's commands? How can you think of such a thing? That I shall never do!"

Since Vesper's judgment is usually excellent, I must have been beside myself to dispute it, but the notion of allowing Helvitius to have his way was altogether repugnant.

"Calm down, Brinnie." Vesper laid a hand on my arm. "We aren't going to sit and do nothing."

"But—dear girl, you just implied that we would follow his instructions."

"He told us not to leave the palace. At the proper time, he'd let Aunt Mary go."

"Do you trust him, then, to keep his word?"

"Of course not," said Vesper. "I don't trust him in anything. There's no telling what he's likely to do. I've been trying to figure it out.

"One sure thing," Vesper went on, "he's in Drackenberg with some scheme up his sleeve. It has to be so important that he can't risk our butting in. He told us as much.

"He must have decided that simply warning us wasn't enough, so he tried to blow us up. That didn't work. All right then, what was the best way to keep us on our good behavior and out of his affairs? Kidnapping Aunt Mary.

"And that," Vesper added, "is where things get very tricky. Once he's finished whatever he's up to, will he really send her back? He might. It's possible. So, if we disobey him, will we be putting her in worse danger?"

"Dear girl, are you telling me we dare do nothing one way or the other?"

Vesper shook her head. "He wants us to stay in the palace. Very well. Let him think so. Let him believe we're doing as he says. Meantime, what we'll really do is start searching for Aunt Mary."

Once again, Vesper's lucid intelligence had resolved an impossible problem. I detected only one flaw: There was no way we could be in two places at once.

"Not easily," Vesper admitted, "but I think we can trick him. For a while, anyway. I don't know how long it will be until he catches on, so we'll have to move fast."

She turned to Duchess Mitzi. "I'm going to assume he has people watching the palace. For all I know, he could have bribed some of your attendants. Do you have any servants you can absolutely rely on?"

"I do," replied Her Highness. "But, child, I must agree with Professor Garrett. There's no way—"

"Have the servants you trust keep on bringing our meals as if we were still here," Vesper pressed on. "I don't want anyone inside or outside the Albertine to suspect we're gone."

"Gone?" I broke in. "Gone where? You said yourself we haven't the slightest clue."

"We might have one," Vesper said. "Mineral water."

"Dear girl, what can mineral water have to do with kidnapping?"

"Maybe a lot." Vesper went to a side table and picked up her Baedeker. "Everything else is in here. There ought to be something about Nymphenwasser."

"That foul-tasting concoction?" put in Duchess Mitzi. "I can tell you all you want to know. For the sake of my liver, I've had to drink more than my share of that disgusting brew. It comes from only one place: Nymphenbaden Spa."

"Right here in Baedeker," Vesper confirmed. "Nymphenbaden Spa. Noted for curative waters, hot pools, sulfur springs."

"As vile-smelling as any in Europe," said Duchess Mitzi. "I've gone there once and have no intention of returning."

"It has a sanatorium for resident patients." Vesper closed the book. "That's not much different from a fancy prison, when you come right down to it. A good place to keep somebody."

"Of course it is!" I exclaimed. "They've locked up Mary there. I know it!"

"I don't," replied Vesper. "The wagon came *from* Nymphenbaden. We can't be sure it's going back. Helvitius is too careful. He wouldn't leave a clue like that. Or—would he?

"Talk about our trying to fool him," Vesper went on. "Is he doing the same to us? Does he want us to think Aunt Mary's in Nymphenbaden, while he's hidden her someplace else? Does he count on us ignoring his orders? Whatever he's up to, my guess is that he needs time. Is he making us waste our own time by sending us on a wild-goose chase?"

Vesper's anxieties were well founded. The villain's mental processes were as devious as they were evil. How could anyone, even Vesper, follow their twisted path?

"We can't outguess him," Vesper said. "So, there's no use trying. All we can do is what makes sense to us."

Finally, I grasped the essence of the dear girl's brilliant plan. While Helvitius was duped into believing us still in the palace, we would go secretly to Nymphenbaden. To my surprise, Vesper did not look at all pleased with herself.

Usually, when the dear girl comes up with one of her schemes she demonstrates enthusiasm and eagerness to get it under way. Now, instead, she appeared strangely thoughtful, even unhappy.

"Brinnie," she said, "I'm not sure what we ought to do."

Such an admission coming from Vesper was bewildering. I could not recall a time when the dear girl had ever been uncertain about anything. Her customary decisiveness seemed to have wilted, her usually bright features clouded with a painful expression, as if she had encountered a dilemma her mental powers could not resolve.

"I don't want Helvitius to get away with this," she said, in a rather forlorn voice. "But—Brinnie, what's im-

61

portant is Aunt Mary. Her life's at stake. If we make one wrong move, we can't tell what may happen to her. It's a risk either way. But which is worse? And which is best for Aunt Mary?"

I understood her hesitation. Indeed, I shared her anguish. We dared not take chances with Mary's life. And yet, we must. Neither of us spoke for some long, hard moments.

"Dear girl," I said at last, "let the decision be mine. Helvitius has lied to us before, he will lie to us again. No matter what he promises, I do not believe he will release Mary. He has led us to assume she is alive. Is this yet another lie? Even as we speak, she might be—"

I could not bring myself to continue that dreadful line of reasoning, so I hastily concluded: "We shall go to Nymphenbaden. On that I am determined. Duchess Mitzi, I trust, will obtain a carriage and driver for us. Inspector Lenz can provide a few of his best officers."

"You'll have all you want," put in Duchess Mitzi, who had been following our discussion intently, as concerned as we were over Mary's plight.

"Yes, but carriages and policemen are just what we don't want," said Vesper. "Nymphenbaden's a good couple of days from Belgard. If we're that long on the open road, there's too much chance we'll be seen and recognized. We don't know how many people Helvitius has watching us or where they are."

Vesper strode up and down, turning the problem over in her mind. Now that we had made our decision, she had stifled her fears and doubts and regained her customary vigor in attacking any question.

"If we want Helvitius to think we're still here," she went on, "the first thing is to get away from the palace without being noticed. That could be hard enough to begin with. Then, to stay unnoticed for a few days—"

I suggested false beards and green spectacles, but Vesper waved away my proposal.

"Simpler than that," she said. "Something Helvitius won't expect. There's a way of getting to Nymphenbaden and back, and it's right in Duchess Mitzi's deer park."

This perplexed me. I could imagine nothing that would serve our purpose, certainly not a herd of horned ruminants.

"Zoltan's caravan," said Vesper. "The Gypsies."

9

"The Gypsies come and go wherever they please," Vesper said. "Zoltan called them children of the wind. People must be used to seeing them wandering around. Nobody's going to give them a second thought."

True, I admitted, but I questioned whether children of the wind would be a reliable mode of transportation.

"I don't see a better choice," replied Vesper. "The only thing is, will Zoltan agree?"

"He'd better agree," Duchess Mitzi said. "I've got that rogue out of more than one scrape. My law protects the Gypsies, but some of the country folk, I'm sorry to say, don't always obey it. They can turn nasty with Gypsies. In one village, they tried to hang Zoltan. If I hadn't got wind of it and saved his neck— Yes, you can be sure he'll do what I ask."

Without further discussion, Duchess Mitzi ordered a servant to fetch the *barossan*. Zoltan did not arrive as quickly as might be expected in answer to her command.

When he did come swaggering in, his appearance was quite different from what it had been at our first meeting. He had put off his finery and, instead of his dazzling jacket, wore a coarse and somewhat threadbare shirt. His only colorful item of apparel was an orange head scarf which made him look as much a grizzled pirate as the leader of a Gypsy *kumpania.* He was, I supposed, dressed in his workaday clothing.

"You summoned me, great *rawnie?* I, Zoltan *barossan,* am at your service. A short service, I hope. We soon head south." He flashed his gold tooth at Duchess Mitzi. "But my heart will yearn for you at every passing mile. And you"—he turned to Vesper—"I will see your face in the flames of our campfire."

"Enough of your eyewash," said Her Highness. "I want a favor."

"Whatever it may be, name it." Zoltan laid a hand in the general vicinity of his heart. "Ask what you will. The moon, the stars, anything—"

"Take Miss Holly and the professor to Nymphenbaden," said Maria-Sophia.

"—anything but that," Zoltan corrected himself hurriedly, adding to Vesper, "If you and the *lavengro* wish a tour of Drackenberg, and certainly it is lovely this time of year, let me suggest any number of other ways. My caravan? No, in all honesty I cannot recommend that. For one thing, we go south, not north. For another: To sleep on the hard ground? Eat what little comes to hand? For us—ah, well, we *rom* are used to it. But not for *gorgios.*"

"*Gorgio* has nothing to do with it."

"Of course not, of course not." Zoltan waved his hands. He gave Vesper a look of wounded innocence. "I do not mean to offend you. Could you have thought for an instant—no, of course you could not—that I bear the least ill will against *gorgios*? Well, yes, it is true, some of them tried to hang me. But I, Zoltan *barossan,* generously forgave them. Out of gratitude to the great *rawnie.*"

"As you well remember," Duchess Mitzi said pointedly. Without mincing further words, she explained what had happened to Mary and our urgent need to go unobserved.

"A serious business," Zoltan said. "For you," he added to Vesper, "perhaps a very dangerous business."

"But you'll take us," Vesper said.

Zoltan did not answer. He looked up at the ceiling and rubbed a hand over his jaw for a while.

"As a favor to Her Highness," Vesper suggested.

"Favors, favors," muttered Zoltan. "I'd have been better hanged. But—no.

"Not as a favor," he went on. "I will take you because—because you are a brave *chai*? Because you go risking your life?" He blew out his breath and shrugged his shoulders. "Because you have green eyes? Who knows? What difference does it make? One foolish reason is as good as another."

"Go safely," Duchess Mitzi said to Vesper. "Go carefully. I won't have an easy stomach until you're back again."

The two of them stood there a moment, eyes meeting, as if the throne of Drackenberg recognized the flower of Philadelphia. The features of the crusty old monarch softened. Duchess Mitzi stumped toward Vesper and put her arms around her.

"If I were twenty years younger—no, five years younger—I'd go with you." She grinned at Vesper. "You might need a dragon."

"Quickly," said Zoltan. "I could change my mind."

The *barossan* led us to the Albertine's deer park. Some very handsome horses had been tethered among the trees. There were four wagons: two canvas covered, the others roofed with wood. A couple of cook fires smoldered. An oldster with an enormous white mustache was hunkered down by one of them, eating with his fingers from a chipped basin. Otherwise, there was an amount of cheerful bustling as Zoltan's *kumpania* made ready to travel.

Except for Vesper's trusty Baedeker, we had brought no luggage. Zoltan had agreed to provide what little we needed for a short space of time.

"If you travel with us," he said, "you'd better look like us. As much as you can, anyway."

We had halted at the largest caravan, a vehicle elaborately carved with horses' heads and painted with odd designs, a battered lantern hanging beside the little step at the doorsill. This *vardo*, Zoltan told us, was his own accommodation. He whistled through his teeth. The door clicked open and out popped a girl no more than nine or ten years old. She was dressed like all the Gypsy women: long skirts, gold hoops in her ears, a dozen strings of beads and chains around her slender neck. Two braids fell past her shoulders; her huge eyes were blacker than her hair and glowed like a coal fire.

"Your daughter?" asked Vesper.

"Mikalia? She is everybody's daughter," said Zoltan. "She has no parents. Since I am the *barossan,* I stand in their place."

The girl stared at us with, to say the least, an expression of displeasure and directed a fast flood of Romany at Zoltan. Vesper inquired if anything was amiss.

"She only wants to know why I brought *gorgios* into our camp," Zoltan replied. "She says I must be out of my wits." He shrugged. "She may be right."

Zoltan set about wheedling and cajoling—to give him credit, he was good at it—until Mikalia's honey-colored features broke into a half smile.

"Come, little one," he said. "Give the *rawnie* and the *lavengro* a nice *choomer.*"

What a *choomer* might be I had no idea until Mikalia came up and planted a very hasty and very wet kiss on my cheek, for which I duly thanked her.

Zoltan's eyes were quicker than mine. As Mikalia turned away, he shot out one hand to seize her shoulder and, with the other, rummaged in the folds of her skirts.

"I think this is yours, *lavengro,*" he said, returning my watch.

"Little imp!" I cried. "She picked my pocket!"

"Very neatly, too," Vesper said, with admiration. "She's a fast one."

Much heated talk followed between Zoltan and Mikalia before she spun away and darted into the caravan.

"A slight misunderstanding," Zoltan explained. "A *gorgio* outside our camp—ah, well, that's fair game. A guest among us, a matter of sacred honor. She did not understand you will be traveling with us, so she believed she had every right. Even so, *lavengro,* a little watch is no great matter. She will not do it again. Probably."

The *barossan* now called over an abundantly proportioned woman, whom he addressed as Rosika, and put Vesper in her charge. Then he instructed Tibor, the white-mustached oldster, to fit me out with suitable clothing. Our opinions on suitability differed, for Tibor dredged up an ancient and extremely unwashed shirt, a sash, and a pair of ragged trousers a few sizes too small in the waist. After I struggled into these garments, Zoltan looked me up and down and appeared more or less satisfied.

Vesper, meantime, had put on a velveteen jacket and breeches, and a pair of soft boots. She had tied her hair under a head scarf and topped it with a crumpled felt hat. Zoltan, hands on hips, inspected the result.

"Are you sure you have no Gypsy blood, *rawnie?* Now you look like a real *romani chal.* I even think you could learn to be one, if you wished."

Knowing Vesper, I had no doubt of that. I only wondered what they would say in Philadelphia.

≈ 10 ≈

Zoltan was anxious for us to be on our way; the sooner done with our business, the sooner he could get about his own. He made an odd little sound with his lips. His horse, browsing some distance away, left off immediately and trotted to him, tossing its mane and nuzzling him.

Vesper, unwilling to be cooped up inside the caravan, preferred sitting outside next to our driver—Mikalia. I joined them, keeping a firm hand on my watch. Despite Vesper's attempt at conversation, the child ignored us. As the *vardo* moved out of the deer park, Vesper noticed a number of sleek little black-and-white birds fluttering along with us.

"Wagtails," said Vesper, never mistaken in her ornithology.

"*Romani chiriklo,*" said Zoltan. "The bird of the *rom.* When you see them, you will find Gypsies close by." He whistled at them, and I could have sworn one of them whistled back at him.

Leaving the palace, Vesper expected Zoltan to pass through Ritterhof Square and make straight for Nymphenbaden. But that, the *barossan* explained, might attract too much attention in such a public place. If Helvitius had set out watchers, the less we were seen the better. We would stay on this side of the river and keep within the protective fringes of the Sommerwald, crossing over later.

The long stretch of woodland making up the Sommerwald began in the city itself, where it was more park than forest, and we passed through it rapidly. Zoltan, trotting his horse beside our caravan, guided us along a fairly smooth forest track. The further from the city, the more his spirits rose.

"So, we head north instead of south. What does it matter, as long as we move?" he said to Vesper. "Your houses are no better than prisons. The *vardo* is our freedom. It moves when and where we please. Can you understand, *rawnie*? We are happy with little, we want for nothing—and so we have everything."

"That's what Epicurus says," replied Vesper.

"That is what Zoltan *barossan* says," declared Zoltan, "and so it is true."

He wheeled his horse and rode to the rear of the caravan, where Tibor had been lagging behind. Vesper looked thoughtfully after him.

"He knows more than we do," she murmured.

If she counted his knack for talking to horses and birds, I agreed.

"He knows how to be free. The *rom* are their own people," Vesper said wistfully. "They're a law unto themselves."

I could have said likewise about Vesper, but I did see what she meant. Our *vardo* was a movable island, following its own path; the rest of the world might as well not have existed, as the iron-shod wheels rolled almost noiselessly over the carpet of pine needles. The light faded; a blue mist drifted through the trees. The lanterns of the caravan bobbed and swung like fireflies. All that was lacking for my peace of mind was the presence of my dear Mary.

Though Zoltan had not gone as far as he had hoped, nightfall obliged us to halt and make camp. Instead of sleeping in the caravans, the Gypsies began pitching small canvas tents.

"Even on the road, we do not like to be shut in," the *barossan* explained. "We sleep in the *vardo* only in the worst of winter, sometimes not then. Weather? What difference does it make? We are friends with all the seasons."

He produced some flexible willow rods and quickly set up our shelter. Mikalia had gone off to join Rosika, who had lit a cook fire. After a time, Zoltan beckoned us over to the fire, where the rest of his band had gathered.

Gorgios though we were, the Gypsies tolerated us, except for little Mikalia, whose occasional glances made me want to check the contents of my pockets. Rosika brought us tin plates of quite a tasty *gulyás,* which Vesper attacked with her customary vigor.

Whatever their opinion of us, Vesper made herself at ease amid the *rom,* sitting with her knees under her chin, her felt hat cocked back on her head. The Gypsies themselves were in good spirits, laughing and joking with one another. Old Tibor had taken his fiddle to strike up one of those yearning, melancholy tunes which, in some contrary way, only made the *rom* all the happier.

Yes, if truth be told, it was not at all bad; not those moments, in any case, with the pungent smell of the fire, Tibor scraping his fiddle, the stars bright and enormous. Had it not been for the urgency of our mission, I believe Vesper could have forgotten all about Philadelphia.

I shall not dwell on my own state of mind. Not wishing to distress the dear girl by adding my anxieties to hers, I resolved to keep up an attitude of confident optimism. Still, when we finished our meal and went back to our tent, I could not conceal my heavyheartedness.

Vesper is not usually given to reproaching herself, but as we settled into our shelter, she sat peering out at the darkness.

"We'll find her," Vesper said. "I only wish I hadn't talked you both into coming. That's my fault, Brinnie."

"Dear girl, you couldn't have known," I assured her. "How could anyone?"

"We'll have her back with us." Vesper laid a hand on my arm. "My dear old Brinnie. I promise you."

When Vesper sets her mind on something, it is as good as done. I could only hope it would be true in this case. I would have been less confident had I known what lay in store, so it was just as well I did not.

Vesper was up and busy by the time I crawled out of the tent, helping to douse the cook fires and pack the gear. She was impatient to be on our way. Zoltan, she told me, planned to cross the branch of the Presta that flowed nearby. He knew of a bridge that would save us many hours of travel. The *barossan,* however, did not appear especially eager to use it.

"Yes, well, you see, *rawnie,*" he said, rubbing his jaw, "that way takes us through the village where they tried to hang me. I forgave them for that. Whether they forgave me, that's something else again."

"They know it's against the law to harm your people, don't they?" said Vesper.

"Tell me about *gorgio* law," Zoltan muttered. He brightened a little. "Still, who remembers a stolen chicken? Or was it a horse? I forget already."

As it turned out, the villagers had longer memories than the *barossan.* The caravan reached the narrow stone bridge within an hour after breaking camp. By then, the locals must have got wind of Gypsies in the vicinity, for a band of them were already lounging in the middle of the span, and a disagreeable-looking group they were. At sight of Zoltan's *vardo,* they began shouting at us, brandishing sticks, and shaking their fists. I had the strong impression they did not want us to cross.

"That's ridiculous," Vesper declared, as Mikalia halted our caravan. "We're only passing through."

Zoltan had ridden up beside us. "You explain that to them, *rawnie,*" he remarked sourly. "You'll see if they have a mind to listen."

"I will." Vesper jumped down from the *vardo* and strode to the bridge. Zoltan dismounted and followed, warning her to be careful. I hurried after them. I had seen my share of ugly crowds. They are much alike, wherever they are, and it takes little to set them off.

Vesper's powers of persuasion are formidable, but the

dear girl had no opportunity to apply them. Before she came within hailing distance, the villagers edged forward and some of the louts began throwing stones.

"Yai!" Zoltan cursed between his teeth. "That rock nearly hit me. Get away from here, *rawnie.* Nothing good will come of this."

I wholeheartedly agreed with him. So far, the villagers had been content merely to block our way. There was no telling whether that would satisfy them or whether they might decide to attack. Between us, Zoltan and I pulled Vesper out of range.

"They're just being spiteful," she cried indignantly, trying to shake loose of us.

"And succeeding," Zoltan muttered.

"Why?" Vesper returned. She glanced over her shoulder. A few more local bullies had joined their companions. "We won't bother them. Why should they act that way?"

"Because we exist," Zoltan burst out angrily. "Because they can never master us. As long as we dance and sing for them, make trained bears of ourselves, tell their fortunes—yes, they tolerate us. This is not true of Duchess Mitzi, but most of the *gorgios* see us as amusements, not humans. They laugh at us or hang us as their fancy strikes them.

"But we are the *rom.* We are free and they are not." Zoltan snorted. "Listen to me, *rawnie.* We are not cowards. Even old Tibor can give a good account of himself. We could try to force our way across. But then we would still have the village to pass through, with those yokels at our heels. How many of the villagers would join them?

75

How should I know? Do you want me to go and ask them?

"You choose, *rawnie*. Shall we fight our way across? The *gorgios* do not frighten me. Slice up a *rom*, you only make ten more."

"No," said Vesper. "What you have is one dead Gypsy."

"That, too," admitted Zoltan.

"I won't let you fight your way through," Vesper said. "There has to be something safer."

"Yes," said Zoltan. "There is another bridge further upstream."

"That's it, then," said Vesper. "Easy. Why didn't you tell me right off?"

"Yes, well, I should also tell you," said Zoltan, "that bridge is a full day's travel from here. Maybe more. But not less."

"We'd lose that much time?" Vesper said. "No, not if we can help it. What we'll have to do is find a shallow place nearby and ford it, wagons and all."

"You know such a place?" Zoltan retorted. "Tell me where it is."

To that, Vesper had no quick answer. However, at her insistence, we turned away from the bridge—while the louts hooted and crowed triumphantly over their victory—and the caravan followed along the river until we were safely out of the villagers' sight. They were satisfied at having so maliciously thwarted the Gypsies, and gave no sign of harassing us beyond their own boundaries.

Vesper, who had been carefully observing the river, soon called out for Zoltan to halt. She had, she told him, found a spot that might be fordable. The *barossan* went with her to examine it, but after one glance turned away.

"It cannot be done," he flatly declared. "Not here. For that matter, not anywhere."

"We can't lose more time," Vesper countered. "It's the best place I've seen. The wagons will float if the water's too deep. The horses can swim."

"Yes, *rawnie,* but not the rest of us."

"You mean you don't know how?" Vesper was astonished. "I thought everybody—"

"We are children of the wind, not the water," replied Zoltan, looking unhappily at the stream. "A *rom* would rather be hanged than drowned."

Zoltan's unwillingness puzzled me; for, in fact, Vesper's keen eye had fallen on a very likely place. The banks were fairly clear of undergrowth and not too steep, and the river itself not forbiddingly wide. To confirm her judgment, Vesper strode without hesitation into the current. She continued until the water reached her waist, paddled a short distance, and soon gained the opposite shore.

There, she waved her arms and beckoned to us. Seeing that Zoltan only stood glumly watching, making no attempt to bring across the caravan, Vesper plunged into the river and came back to us.

Without belittling any of the dear girl's remarkable accomplishments, I must in all honesty admit that this was one of her less spectacular. In El Dorado, Vesper had confronted the treacherous waters of the Rio Culebra; in comparison, I doubted that the gentler waterways of Drackenberg could offer much challenge. Joining us, soaking wet and shaking herself like a spaniel, she was barely winded and had even retained her felt hat.

"It's only deep in a couple of places." Vesper grinned

and wiped her brow. "Some rocks here and there. The wagons won't have any trouble."

"You expect me to try that?" Zoltan grimaced. "Don't ask."

"No," said Vesper. "I'll do it."

Zoltan refused point-blank. Since Vesper's power of persuasion had not been used against the village louts, it had, as it were, built up a head of steam and she now turned it on the *barossan*. Zoltan certainly was a strong-willed and long-seasoned fellow; not for nothing was he leader of his *kumpania*. But the poor man had no chance against Vesper at her most effective, and he finally threw up his hands.

"Go and wreck my *vardo*," he cried. "Swamp us, flood us out. Why do I listen to a green-eyed *gorgio*? Who knows? Who cares anymore?"

Given that enthusiastic approval, Vesper set about convincing the others. She was not as successful as she had been with Zoltan, so the unhappy *barossan* found himself in the awkward position of having to browbeat Rosika, Tibor, and the rest into climbing aboard their *vardos*.

They crouched there, clinging to the sides of the wagons, like castaways in a lifeboat expecting to founder at any moment. Nevertheless, once Vesper had driven the first *vardo* into the river, slapping the reins, urging the struggling horse, and finally gaining the opposite bank, the rest of the *rom* grew a little more confident. I would not go so far as to say they enjoyed it, but they put up with it.

Having landed the first one safely, Vesper swam back and did likewise with the next wagon, and again with the third. Zoltan's *vardo* was last, the *barossan* claiming it was his responsibility to see his people safe before he risked his own neck.

With little Mikalia perched on the roof and Zoltan in front beside us, muttering to himself, Vesper unhesitatingly drove into the current. By this time, the dear girl had become quite skillful at ferrying.

But then, as ill luck would have it, one of the wheels must have jammed against a rock. The *vardo* stopped short in midstream, the horse tossed its dripping mane, neighed fearfully, and refused to budge.

From the shore, the Gypsies shouted in alarm, whistled, and called out, making every effort to coax the animal into motion. Zoltan himself clicked his tongue, whispered, pleaded, and burst into a string of Romany endearments—or curses, for all I could understand of that colorful tongue. The horse laid back its ears and ignored the desperate *barossan*.

"I thought the *rom* could talk to horses," remarked Vesper.

"We can," retorted Zoltan. "He's not listening."

Vesper added her voice to the *barossan*'s. Since Romany had failed, she tried French, German, and Italian. None of these brought any response. We moved neither forward nor backward. Mikalia, atop the *vardo,* had begun whimpering, and the despairing Zoltan clapped his hands to his head.

Vesper, of course, is fluent in most languages. By now, though, I feared she had exhausted her vocabulary. Suddenly, her eyes lit up and she launched into the majestic cadences of classic Greek, declaiming passages from what I immediately recognized as the *Iliad*.

The horse pricked up its ears. Zoltan, open-mouthed,

stared at her as she continued to ring out those mighty lines, while the animal reared and snorted and began to heave with all its strength.

"*Rawnie,* what is this?" Zoltan cried in astonished admiration. "Where have you learned such power? Even I, Zoltan *barossan,* know nothing like it."

"I got it from Homer," Vesper answered.

"Homer?" Zoltan raised his eyebrows. "A horse trader?"

"An old poet."

"Also a *rom?*"

"He wandered a lot," said Vesper.

Zoltan nodded. "Clearly, one of us."

Before Vesper could explain, the *vardo* lurched ahead. The Gypsies whooped and cheered as the horse plunged through the current. The *vardo* swayed and tilted as the water seized it.

Then a sudden jolt sent Mikalia screaming headlong into the river.

CHAPTER

≈ **11** ≈

Vesper flung me the reins, for there was no stopping the horse now, and Zoltan jumped to his feet despite the lurching of the *vardo*. For all his inability to swim, he would surely have bravely tried to do so. But Vesper moved faster than the *barossan*. While I could do no more than let the horse make for dry ground, Vesper plunged after the screaming Mikalia.

The current had borne the child into the deepest eddies of the river. The Gypsies ran along the bank, and some even ventured hopelessly into the shallows. Vesper's powerful strokes soon brought her within reach of Mikalia, who was choking and wailing at the same time. The terrified little girl so struggled, flailing her arms and legs, that I feared Vesper, strong swimmer though she was, might never bring her ashore.

The two of them bobbed and spun like a couple of corks. For an instant, both disappeared below the surface. But Vesper found her footing again and, with Mikalia clutched in her arms, stumbled up the sloping riverbank.

The cheering Gypsies crowded around them. Vesper gave the sobbing child into the abundant embrace of Rosika. Zoltan, assured that the girl was unharmed, his *kumpania* safe, and the horses equally so, beamed and swaggered about as if the whole enterprise had been his idea. Yet he did not neglect to give Vesper her full share of praise.

"You saved the life of a *rom,*" he cried, throwing his arms about Vesper. "A small *rom,* but that makes no difference. It is still a big debt."

He took a gold chain and amulet from his neck. "*Rawnie,* I, Zoltan *barossan,* give you my prized possession. But even that is worth less than what you have done."

Vesper, always becomingly modest on such occasions, admired the gift but did not wish to deprive Zoltan of a priceless heirloom.

"You must accept it," the *barossan* insisted. "It is a matter of honor. Besides," he added, "I have extras in the wagon."

Mikalia, during this, had wiggled free of Rosika and went shyly to Vesper. The child hesitated, then, as Vesper grinned at her, suddenly ran to let herself be hugged, all the while bestowing a few dozen *choomers* on her rescuer.

At Zoltan's order, Tibor rummaged out a candle and ancient knife from one of the *vardos.* The *barossan* thrust the blade into the ground and lit the candle.

"By fire and iron," Zoltan declared, "what we agree here is binding on all the *pralos,* all our brethren. It was not your fault that you were born a *gorgio,* so we shall change that. From now on, we count you as one of us.

You, too, *lavengro*," he added. "For the sake of the *rawnie*, who has done us a great service."

Whether it occurred to Zoltan that he would not have needed Vesper's help if she had not entangled him in her plan to begin with, I do not know. But I doubted it. The dear girl has a way of turning things around, which can be confusing. It is one of her many charms.

In any case, Vesper was much aware of this unusual honor, and so was I: It is rare for a *gorgio* to be considered a Romany *rye,* a true friend of the Gypsies. Vesper made a graceful speech of acceptance, I added a few words of my own, and we received the embraces of all the *kumpania.* In Philadelphia, it would have been comparable to election to our noble Athenaeum.

We set off, then. This time, instead of riding in sullen silence, little Mikalia never stopped chattering to Vesper. At our occasional halts, the girl was constantly at Vesper's side, her enormous black eyes glowing with admiration. Zoltan himself looked on the dear girl with nothing short of amazement and perhaps even a degree of adoration. She could have invented the steam engine and he would have shrugged that off: It was Vesper's horsemanship that did it.

The *barossan* more than made up for lost time. We crossed the Presta—happily, without interference—before dark, and made camp in a woodland only a couple of miles from Nymphenbaden.

The *kumpania* would have celebrated their two new members with dancing and fiddle music, but Vesper had more serious concerns. With Mikalia at her side as usual, she called the Gypsies to gather around her at the campfire so that she could talk over our plans for the next day.

"We can't just pull up to Nymphenbaden in a caravan," she began. "We'd be grateful for your help, but Brinnie and I will do better on our own. I thought about sneaking into the spa at night, but that could be too risky. Then I wondered if Brinnie could let on to be an invalid coming to take the waters. He could be suffering from gout or some such. But we'd need a wheelchair."

"I can get one for you," put in Mikalia. "I'll find a village and *chore* anything you want."

"So she could," said Zoltan. "She's small, but she's quick."

"No," said Vesper, "the simplest thing would be to say we're touring the countryside and we'd like to sample the mineral water, the baths, or whatever. If we do that, we'll need our regular clothes back again."

"For you, *rawnie,* I can do something better." Zoltan hustled to his *vardo* and soon came back with an assortment of secondhand lederhosen, jackets, heavy loden cloaks, hobnailed boots, rucksacks, caps, and walking staffs.

"Exactly right," said Vesper, delighted with the costumes. "We'll be on a walking tour. Who'll think twice when we show up there on foot?"

Zoltan's wagon must have held an infinite number of odds and ends, for he now offered us the use of an antique blunderbuss and a pair of Heidelberg dueling sabers. But Vesper refused them.

"We're only going to have a look around," she said. "If we don't run into trouble, we won't need them. If we do run into trouble, they can't help us much."

She was, of course, absolutely right.

We awoke early next morning. Vesper awoke, that is. My night was sleepless. Zoltan and Mikalia would gladly have gone with us all the way to the spa, but Vesper advised against it.

"I don't know what we'll find, if anything," she said, "or what we'll do if it turns out Aunt Mary's there. I'd rather have you here in case we need you later. One way or another, we should be back before nightfall."

Zoltan reluctantly agreed, but he and Mikalia insisted on going with us to the edge of the woodland. There we halted while Mikalia gave us a couple of *choomers* and the *barossan* embraced Vesper.

"*Bahtalo drom,*" he said. "Travel a good road."

Mikalia, I think, would have followed us if Zoltan had not picked her up and put her on his shoulder. They turned back to the camp while Vesper and I continued in the direction of the spa.

Vesper strode out briskly, plying her staff as the road turned steeper. It ran uphill most of the way, sloping downward only after we came in sight of Nymphenbaden. We were, in fact, among the foothills of the Carlomanians, with the snow-capped Drackenberg, which had given the grand duchy its name, looming ahead seemingly within hand's reach.

In happier circumstances, I might have found our walk pleasantly bracing, for the sky was bright, the air cooler than in Belgard; the pine forests bordering both sides of the road were peaceful, silent except for the occasional birdsong. For a moment, then, my dear Mary's disappearance seemed only a nightmare, as if I might suddenly wake and find her, as always, at my side.

The closer we drew to Nymphenbaden, the sharper grew my apprehensions. Vesper remained certain that our plan was the best we could devise, though I had begun to distrust the notion of fobbing ourselves off as innocent wayfarers.

"We have to try it," Vesper replied. "I don't see what else we can do."

As it turned out, our arrival presented no difficulties. We were, that morning, not the only visitors to Nymphenbaden. Several carriages had already passed through the iron gates; a horse-drawn omnibus had halted just outside. Its passengers had come for a day's outing, and we were able to mingle with them without drawing any special attention to ourselves.

The largest buildings of the spa, the glass-domed Kursaal and the adjoining sanatorium, rose at the far end of a broad, shrub-lined walkway. Here and there were groves of greenery, stone balustrades, replicas of Greek statuary. It was, however little known, as elegant as any of the more famous watering places on the continent.

"I see what Duchess Mitzi meant about the smell." Vesper sniffed as we approached the Kursaal, where an aroma of sulfur hung in the air. "I suppose you get used to it."

Within the Kursaal, a uniformed attendant directed us to a desk at the end of a marble vestibule. Vesper presented me as a retired banker from the city of New York, and herself as my nephew. With her cap pulled low to hide her hair, the dear girl was altogether convincing in that role. She explained that I had fallen victim to a recurring liver complaint in the course of our walking tour and hoped to gain relief from the curative waters.

Had we claimed to be visiting royalty, the manager could not have been more delighted. There were, he told us, rarely guests from beyond the borders of the grand duchy.

In that case, I put in, he might be aware of any of our compatriots here in residence.

"No, my dear sir," he answered, "we have not been favored by the presence of Americans, except for your honored selves."

When Vesper asked if we might inspect the facilities, he was eager to oblige. He urged us to stroll through the pavilion, to observe the pools and baths at our leisure. Meantime, he would summon the director, who would offer us a complete tour.

Vesper politely thanked him, and we made our way to one of the garden spots. Nearby, a few of the guests sipped glasses of murky water from a fountain. We kept apart from them and sat on a marble bench while Vesper contemplated what information we might draw out of the director.

"Don't be too curious, Brinnie," she said under her breath. "First thing, just let him show us around. If Aunt Mary's here, there could be a dozen places Helvitius might keep her. I want to see what we have to deal with."

She broke off at the approach of a stout, smiling gentleman in a white laboratory coat. His eyes twinkled behind a pair of pince-nez spectacles as he warmly shook our hands and introduced himself as the director, Dr. Tiezor.

"All our facilities are at your disposal," he told us, after declaring himself honored by our patronage. He gestured for us to follow along the pathway. "You may wish to benefit from our full course of treatment—the baths and the dietary regimen—or, if your time is limited, a day or two of mild exercise, purgation, and absorption of our Nymphenwasser.

"We specialize in the liver," he added, glancing at me as I tried to assume a properly jaundiced expression, "and our cures have been most effective."

"I'm sure they have," said Vesper. "First, though, we'd like to see the rest of the spa."

"Of course," replied Dr. Tiezor. "It will be my pleasure to conduct you, Fräulein—"

Dr. Tiezor stopped short. The unintended word had slipped out so naturally that it took me a second to realize he had addressed Vesper with a feminine honorific.

Vesper, however, was instantly aware of the mistake. Before she could make a move, Dr. Tiezor gripped her arm.

"You cannot escape, Fräulein Holly," he muttered between his teeth, all the while maintaining a polite smile. "You will please make no disturbance."

꒛ 12 ꒘

"Won't I?" replied Vesper.

As a medical practitioner, in a position of authority as director of an extensive health resort, Dr. Tiezor might have expected the same docility from Vesper as from his other patients. The dear girl's tendency, in similar circumstances, has always been to the contrary: to make as great a disturbance as possible.

The treacherous director had not reckoned on this aspect of Vesper's personality; nor had he reckoned on her elbow, which she drove with all her might into his midsection.

Dr. Tiezor made wheezing noises and doubled over at the force of Vesper's blow. As far as I was concerned, the director had sacrificed any respect due him as a member of the healing profession. I felt no compunction in bringing up my walking staff and striking him sharply about the head and shoulders. Dr. Tiezor sat down heavily on the gravel.

"Run for it, Brinnie," Vesper suggested.

She took to her heels; I raced after her across the walkway, plunging past a group of guests clustered at one of the medicinal fountains. Some drew back in alarm; most only turned idly curious glances upon us. Patients overstimulated by their treatment were, perhaps, not an uncommon sight at Nymphenbaden.

Dr. Tiezor, meantime, had recovered most of his wits and breath.

"Lunatics!" he shouted. "Dangerous lunatics!"

From the tail of my eye, I glimpsed a trio of whitecoated attendants hastening to answer his summons. Ahead rose a stone balustrade. Vesper clambered over it and dropped to the shrubbery below. We flung off the burden of our rucksacks, and I tumbled into the bushes after her.

"Front gate!" cried Vesper. "Try for it!"

With the attendants behind us, we dared not turn back. Vesper, I realized, was hoping to circle around the Kursaal and sanatorium; yet neither of us was familiar enough with the grounds to choose the quickest route. With my own sense of direction confused, I could only follow as Vesper burst out of the hedges and raced across the garden bed lining one of the pathways.

Past a rank of statuary, we gained an open expanse of lawn where a party of elderly ladies was playing a quiet game of croquet. Vesper ran straight on, sidestepping or leaping over the wickets marking the course of this genteel recreation.

Alas, I did not do likewise.

At that moment, I ventured a hasty glance over my shoulder, and was dismayed to see two of the attendants closing rapidly upon us. My foot caught in one of the accursed wickets. I went sprawling full length.

When I strove to regain my legs, my ankle twisted and I stumbled to the ground again. The attendants were upon me. Vesper, hearing my outcry, halted and turned back. I shouted for her to save herself and make good her escape. Dear, gallant girl! Even as they seized me, she threw herself on my captors, fighting to pull me free of their grasp.

Her efforts were in vain. By now, another pair of Dr. Tiezor's hirelings had come running from the opposite direction. Behind them, looking far from benign, was Dr. Tiezor himself.

The ladies broke off their game. One, in a large, flowered hat, stepped forward.

"The gentleman," she observed, "appears to be in difficulty."

"Madam, pray continue your recreation." The despicable Tiezor adjusted his pince-nez and assured her and her party there was no cause for concern. The wretch had already violated his Hippocratic oath. To that offense he now added falsehood.

"These unhappy patients," he said smoothly, "suffer from delusions of persecution."

"Persecution is right," retorted Vesper, "but it's no delusion."

"Help us, dear lady," I cried. "My solemn word on it, we are not lunatics, we are Philadelphians!"

All further protest was useless. As I was hauled to my feet, another of Tiezor's staff arrived with some wet sheets. Even Vesper, for all her struggling, could not keep them from swathing us in these restrictive wrappings.

Confinement in the clammy cocoon of a wet sheet is a

demoralizing experience. Vesper, seldom daunted, surely felt as disheartened as I did. While the attendants, at Tiezor's instructions, hustled us toward a back entrance of the sanatorium, Vesper gave up berating them and fell silent. We had no choice but to allow ourselves to be marched down a hallway and into Tiezor's consulting rooms.

Here, added to the ever-present odor of brimstone, was the smell of medical preparations and formaldehyde. Lining the walls were cabinets and shelves cluttered with bottles, surgical instruments, and the usual display of disgusting things in jars, typical of clinical offices even in Philadelphia.

Figged out in gaiters and a shooting jacket, lounging on the examining table, one leg nonchalantly cocked over the other, was Count Bertrand.

"Hallo, what's this?" He waved a hand at us without troubling to remove a thin cigar from between his teeth—the stench of that nauseating weed worse than the formaldehyde—as he added, "Costume party, Tiezor? Got them up like Egyptian mummies?"

Aristocracy does not confer immunity to the law of humanity, and my outrage made me overstep the bounds of civility to which his rank entitled him.

"Scoundrel!" I burst out. "What have you done with my wife? I demand to know. Where is Mrs. Garrett?"

The count blew a smoke ring and contemplated it a moment. "Can't really say. Fact is, I haven't the slightest notion."

"Haven't you?" Vesper flung at him. "You lied when you said you didn't know Helvitius. Don't try to tell me you aren't lying now."

She took a step toward him. Restricted though she was by the sheets, Count Bertrand slid off the table and backed away from her.

"You listen to me," Vesper declared. "You've got Aunt Mary and I want to see her."

"Sorry, can't oblige." Bibi continued to keep a safe distance between himself and Vesper. "The matter's entirely out of my hands."

"Don't ask us to swallow that." Vesper's eyes flashed at him. "You're not here for the mineral water. And you're certainly not shooting snipe. You were expecting us. The first place we'd look for her—"

She broke off suddenly. The dear girl rarely makes a mistake in her calculations, mathematical or otherwise, but now she turned to me and murmured, "Is he telling the truth? Aunt Mary isn't here? I wondered if Helvitius was sending us on a wild-goose chase. It isn't. It's a trap." She fixed her glance again on Bibi.

"All right, then. Where's Helvitius? You've cooked this up with that murderous villain."

"Murderous? Well, yes, he can be a bit overbearing." Bibi puffed away on his noxious cheroot. "Still, he's been doing first-rate service for Carpatia. Cousin Rudi thinks rather fondly of him. Recommended the chap to me, in fact. I'm counting on him to put a few pennies in the old money box. And something a little better, too. But I haven't seen him . . . recently. He goes about his own business."

"And your business," Vesper snapped. "You're in this, Bibi. Whatever it is, you won't get away with it."

Helpless though she was, Vesper's blunt words reflected my own outrage. Given the use of my hands, I would have had them at the throat of this pomaded sprig.

"You, sir, may choose not to answer us," I said sharply, "but sooner or later you shall answer to the law."

"Me? To some dull-witted detectives in ready-made suits? You forget I'm a member of the royal family." Bibi gave a most irritating and supercilious smile.

"Sir," I replied, "I refer to a higher justice. No one is beyond its reach."

Bibi merely shrugged. He glanced at Dr. Tiezor. "I'll want a couple of words with you later. Get on with it, Tiezor. But don't expect me to watch."

Bibi tossed his cheroot to the floor and sauntered past us. At the door, he turned and waved. "Should I say *auf Wiedersehen*? I suppose not. I won't be seeing you again."

"Come back here, you sneaking little weasel!" Vesper would have set off after him if the attendants had not restrained her.

Dr. Tiezor had gone to his medical cabinet and taken out a large hypodermic syringe.

"You, sir," I demanded, "what are you—"

Before I could say more, or attempt to break away from my captors, I felt the sting of the needle in my arm.

Dr. Tiezor approached Vesper. I cried out and tried to fight my way to her side. The room had begun to swim around me. Catching a last glimpse of Vesper's face, I dimly heard the dear girl call to me, and nothing beyond that.

⇒ 13 ⇐

By and large, it was not unpleasant and, sometimes, rather happy.

My dear Mary was there. Vesper was strumming her banjo while Moggie the cat served tea and fish paste sandwiches. My old companion Holly himself arrived, bearded, wearing a sola topee. We were all delighted to be together, laughing, chatting, enjoying the fish paste.

But that scene gave way to a continual, jolting blackness. I cried out, trying to summon my dear ones back again.

"Brinnie? Can you sit up?"

I experienced a feeling of satisfaction mixed with surprise. I thought the situation over carefully and concluded that Vesper was alive and, presumably, so was I. Yet, when the reality was borne in upon me, I would have gladly chosen oblivion.

The dear girl was beside me on what seemed to be a low cot. I think I answered that I preferred to remain horizontal.

"Brinnie, for heaven's sake, will you wake up!"

Dim light came through a small window at the rear of our chamber. It was, in fact, daybreak. As Vesper later reckoned, Dr. Tiezor's injection had been powerful enough to render us unconscious until the following morning.

For me, at the moment, the passage of time had been incalculable, infinite, crowded with disordered recollections. As bits of memory returned, I supposed we had been stored away in a closet in the sanatorium. I could not understand why it seemed to be in motion.

"A first aid chest. Stacks of bandages," Vesper said. "They've put us in an ambulance."

"Have we been ill?" I asked.

With a cry of both impatience and concern, Vesper continued urging me to rouse myself. I saw no reason to do so. I closed my eyes and drifted away. When I opened them again—how much later I did not know—I stared upward into the face of a white-haired old man. He jabbered incomprehensibly. He looked vaguely familiar. Perhaps we had once met on the Spanish Steps in Rome. I asked him about that.

"Brinnie, you've got to pull yourself together," Vesper said, shaking me. "You know Pognor. Don't you understand yet? We're in Schwanfeld Castle."

My astonishment at her words did much to clear my spinning head. I did, at last, manage to sit up. We were not on cots but stretchers, and still wrapped in clammy sheets. I saw nothing of any attendants who had carried us in.

Now that I was fully awake, chilled to the bone despite the blaze in the huge fireplace, I recognized the dining hall, the high, shadowy ceilings, and the massive refectory table we had glimpsed during our first visit.

Old Pognor, bewildered by our presence and strange predicament, was nevertheless delighted to see us. He remembered us, although in a disjointed sort of way. Vesper, once met, is not easily forgotten, but in Pognor's case, I quickly realized the poor chap had difficulty putting his recollections in order. His mind seemed to be a cluttered attic which he wandered through, stumbling over odds and ends of the distant past and immediate present. That, in addition to his inscrutable patois, left me as confused as he was.

In any case, the old retainer beamed and babbled and could not do enough for us. He bent his rickety efforts toward helping Vesper up from the stretcher and performed the same service for me. Vesper urged him to remove our sopping sheets—he thought these were new-style travel costumes and that we had suffered a boating accident. He fumbled at them with every good intention and little result.

"He's sorry Aunt Mary isn't with us," Vesper translated. "She could meet Count Sigismund. From what I make of it, he's in residence now."

"Dear girl," I cried, "we are in safe hands at last! The Karolyi-Walseggs are ancient nobility. They might even be related to Duchess Mitzi. Surely we can rely on young Sigismund to help us. There's no reason on earth why he should wish us ill."

"Then," countered Vesper, "why did we get packed up and sent here? I doubt that it was Bibi's idea. Helvitius must have ordered it."

On second thought, that puzzled me. A moment's reflection gave me the reasonable answer. Helvitius's scheme, whatever it was, had misfired. He and Bibi wanted to get us off their hands quickly. Sigismund and Bibi were doubtless friends. It was perfectly logical to deposit us in Schwanfeld.

"It isn't logical to me," said Vesper. "When Helvitius makes a plan, it doesn't misfire."

She turned to Pognor. "Do you have any idea what's going on? Does the count know we're here?"

"Count Willi?" said Pognor. "I think not. You see, he is no longer alive."

"I understand that," Vesper said patiently. "I'm talking about Count Sigismund. Siggi."

"Ah, Siggi." Pognor shook his head and clicked his tongue. "That Siggi, always such a little scamp. I told him he must not set the cat on fire."

"Of course he mustn't," Vesper agreed. "Now, Pognor—"

"And playing games in the cellars," Pognor went on. "Naughty boy. But Count Willi paid no mind—"

"Pognor," insisted Vesper, "listen to me carefully. Please. Go and fetch Siggi."

"I should go to Paris?" Pognor looked more baffled than ever.

"No," said Vesper. "Here. Schwanfeld. You told us he was in residence."

"Who? The *Meister*?"

"Yes. Your master. The lord of the manor, whatever you call him."

"Ah!" Pognor's face brightened. "Yes. He is here."

"Good," said Vesper. "Now, go and tell Count Siggi—"

"But I cannot do that," Pognor protested.

"Perhaps I can explain it more clearly," said a voice from the doorway.

Wearing a dressing gown and jaunty polka-dot foulard, and looking in the best of spirits, Dr. Helvitius stepped into the dining hall.

14

Vesper had managed to free her arms from the restrictions of the sheet. She started toward Helvitius, who smiled and raised a warning hand.

"My dear Miss Holly," he said, "in our long and often interesting acquaintance, I have not known you to do an unwise thing. I suggest you do not do one now."

Vesper paused, for she had noticed, as I had, two men carrying hunting rifles. The pair had sidled in quietly to stand in the doorway behind Helvitius. In jackets and leggings, they could have passed for gamekeepers. But, to my eye, they were city-bred lurchers, for all their country-style hats with bunches of rooster feathers in the crowns.

Vesper seemed to recognize them, but made no comment. I, too, had the impression I had seen them before. Though my thoughts were still confused by the lingering effect of Tiezor's injection—and more so by the presence of Helvitius—I vaguely recalled one as being among those half-dozen brawlers under arrest in the Belgard police station.

What their association with Helvitius might be, except that one villain gravitates toward another, I could not puzzle out. Given our more urgent concerns, that was hardly a matter of importance.

"Disregard the maunderings of this senile relic." Helvitius gestured at Pognor, who had been observing the scene, frowning and shaking his grizzled head. "On occasion, he mistakes me for the gardener or the bailiff. Alas, he has long outlived his usefulness. I shall have to arrange something for him when I have a spare moment. Dogs"— Helvitius addressed this last to Pognor—"in the kennel! Do you understand? Go and see to them."

While Pognor hobbled out, Helvitius went and spoke apart with his ruffians.

"Don't let on we've been here before," Vesper hurriedly whispered. "I don't know if Pognor's told Helvitius about our visit. I hope not. The less Helvitius knows, the better. But—is Aunt Mary in Schwanfeld? Why did Pognor say he was sorry she wasn't with us? If Helvitius has her in the castle, Pognor would know."

"Would he?" I replied. "His memory's a shambles. We can't rely on anything he tells us."

"True," Vesper admitted. "Even so—"

She stopped when Helvitius returned, looking pleased with himself, as if the wretch had just savored an excellent breakfast and anticipated a still more agreeable day.

"In one regard, the decrepit idiot is correct," said Helvitius. "I am, in every sense, the master here. Schwanfeld is mine. The entire estate, the outlying landholdings as well—and they are not inconsiderable."

"Then you are a usurper," I retorted. "I am given to understand that Count Sigismund is the heir—" I stopped in mid-phrase. A monstrous thought had come to me. "It cannot be possible! That you are—"

"Sigismund?" Helvitius threw back his head and laughed heartily. "My dear Professor, what a marvelous notion! It is too humorous to be insulting." He drew a handkerchief from his sleeve and dabbed his eyes. He chuckled again, finding the idea vastly entertaining. "Any resemblance between myself and that depraved individual—your suggestion is deliciously grotesque."

"Why, then, is he not in possession of his birthright?" I demanded. "Is he another victim of your foul schemes? What have you done to him?"

"What I have done to him," replied Helvitius, "is to make him incredibly rich. He is in Paris, indulging himself in those peculiar pleasures he finds so attractive."

"I know nothing of that young man's way of life," I said coldly, "but it cannot be as despicable as your own. Vile being! To attempt our destruction by means of exploding edibles. What could be more reprehensible! To employ a harmless Drackenbergerwurst as an instrument of murder!"

"One can only do one's best." Helvitius shrugged. "As for Schwanfeld, my dear Professor, I assure you I have done nothing that was not in perfect legal order. I purchased the estate from Count Sigismund.

"My original offer was made to Count Wilhelm, but he refused. I feared I would be compelled to resort to other means. He had the good grace, however, to depart this world—it was none of my doing, you have my word on it. Nevertheless, given the seriousness of my purpose, if need be, I would not have hesitated to speed him on his way.

"Count Sigismund, on the other hand, was overjoyed

to accept. He would have been foolish to turn down my offer, for it was a substantial sum even to one of my own wealth. Paris, City of Light, has ample areas of shadow. He prefers the resources of that great capital to the meagerness of a rustic existence. He has no interest whatever in this garish pile and its collection of absurd trinkets. By taking it off his hands, I did him a service."

"I don't care a rap for your real estate business," put in Vesper. "I want to know what you've done with Aunt Mary."

"Forgive me, Miss Holly," replied Helvitius. "I neglected to congratulate you on your shrewd analysis, incomplete and faulty though it was. I hoped you would assume that Mrs. Garrett had been taken to Nymphenbaden."

"I also assumed you gave us that clue on purpose," Vesper said.

"Indeed I did. I apologize for not being there myself to receive you. Urgent business prevented me. So, I asked Count Bertrand to have you conveyed here."

Helvitius sauntered to the fireplace. He smiled complacently at Vesper. "You are a remarkable young woman, Miss Holly. Alas, we so often find ourselves in opposition."

"Often?" returned Vesper. "Permanently."

"And regrettably. You have the keenest mind of anyone it has been my pleasure to encounter. Your intelligence almost matches my own. In many ways, you are unpredictable. Yet, in others, I understand your mental processes clearly. I expected you to disregard my warning. I expected you to make your way to Nymphenbaden; though how you did so, I have not yet discovered.

"One thing you do not realize," he went on. "Mrs. Garrett is not important to me. Her abduction was only a means of luring you and the professor within my reach. Coincidence brought us together in Drackenberg, but that coincidence offered me an irresistible opportunity. Since my sausage failed to achieve its purpose, I resorted to another plan."

"To perdition with you and your vile plans!" I burst out. "Where, sir, is my wife?"

"Your question is immaterial," Helvitius replied. "It has no bearing on your present circumstances."

"Then, monster," I cried, "tell me at least if she is alive."

"Since you and Miss Holly will soon cease to exist," Helvitius answered, "that question is also immaterial."

"Maybe to us," Vesper calmly replied. "Not to you. The grand duchess knows about you. She'll have you tracked down sooner or later."

"I doubt that," said Helvitius. "In any case, within the near future, Drackenberg will no longer be ruled by a grand duchess."

"Assassin!" Had my arms been disentangled, I would have shaken a fist at him. "I should have known it from the first!"

"Can you believe I would do away, literally, with the charming Maria-Sophia?" Helvitius looked wounded by my accusation. "I would not dream of such a thing. Unless it were necessary. Which it is not. On the contrary, such an act would outrage the populace and that I do not wish. No, sir, my fondest desire is peace. It can often be as profitable as war.

"What I predict with certainty is this: By popular demand—in any case, the appearance of popular demand—King Rudolf will be invited, welcomed, entreated to annex Drackenberg. Maria-Sophia will be, shall we say, encouraged to abdicate. She will spend her few remaining years in more or less comfortable exile. Her successor on the throne, the new grand duke, will be Bertrand."

"Bibi?" cried Vesper. "That weasel? That brainless nitwit?"

"An ideal monarch," said Helvitius. "As long as he is amply rewarded, he will at least be wise enough to keep out of matters that do not concern him. His flaws make him the perfect choice."

"Grand Duke Bibi?" retorted Vesper. "Don't bet on it. That won't ever happen."

"It will, Miss Holly. The movement in favor of annexation will grow stronger day by day. Yes, I am certain it will. For a very simple reason: I am its architect.

"I am the owner, naturally under a different name, of Belgard's most influential newspaper. In addition, those groups of individuals roving the streets—I believe you had a brief experience with some of them—are in my employ. For those services, and others, King Rudolf has agreed—"

"To line your pockets!" I burst out. "Your avarice has made you no more than a hireling, a mercenary!"

"Not at all," replied Helvitius. "My efforts have been undertaken at my own personal and considerable expense. I was about to say that King Rudolf has agreed to grant me certain privileges."

"He must have granted you something," Vesper said.

"What I don't see is why he wants Drackenberg in the first place."

"He wants it very much," said Helvitius, "precisely for what I can provide from the Schwanfeld estates. During my inspection of the properties, I discovered what none of the Karolyi-Walseggs ever knew: Much of the outlying land is richer than anyone could imagine.

"It holds deposits of a substance more precious than gold or silver," Helvitius went on. "I refer, Miss Holly, to bauxite. It is the source of a most remarkable new metal."

"Aluminum," said Vesper. "Yes, it's remarkable. But if that's what you're after, you've wasted your time and money. From what I've read, it's too hard to get aluminum out of the bauxite ore."

"You underestimate my knowledge of metallurgy and electrochemistry," replied Helvitius. "Through my intensive research and experimentation, I alone have discovered a means of extracting it in quantity and even alloying it with other metals.

"I know the secret of producing an aluminum that is light as a feather and strong as steel. King Rudolf has licensed me as his sole supplier. My product will be worth a fortune to him for a myriad of industrial and military purposes. And worth an even greater fortune to me."

"Aluminum—the one thing that would make Drackenberg prosperous," Vesper said bitterly. "And it will all go to Carpatia. Yes, if Rudolf takes over the grand duchy he'll have a gold mine—that is, a bauxite mine—in his backyard."

"That was not my original intention," said Helvitius. "Call it a profitable combination of circumstances, a happy accident. I did not acquire Schwanfeld for its bauxite. I was, at first, unaware of its hidden riches. My purpose was altogether different. Yet, Miss Holly, I assure you I would have paid the same price and more for something I have sought for many years, whose very existence I often doubted.

"Now I possess it. Now it is in my hands. As its owner, I am privileged to name it. I choose to call it *La Fortunata.*"

~ 15 ~

"Another of your diabolical inventions?" I cried. "Some new engine of destruction? We have no interest in your villainous devices."

"Diabolical?" said Helvitius. "On the contrary. Angelic. Sublime. Destruction? No, the highest achievement of human creation. If you are not interested, Miss Holly will surely be.

"You know my passion for music," Helvitius continued. "My passion for art is no less. My private collection holds many masterpieces, yet I would gladly exchange them all for this one. For a long time, I believed it to be only legendary. Or, if it ever existed, to be lost beyond recovery.

"Then, a year ago, a letter came into my possession. As an antiquarian and bibliophile, I recognized it was completely genuine. That document alone would be a prize in itself. What it revealed—I cannot describe my emotions when I understood its significance.

"It was written by a young bride to her cousin. Among other subjects, she refers to a painting she has brought with her to her new household. She narrates in detail the circumstances of its creation, the artist who painted it, and her conversations with him. She expresses her admiration, how greatly she treasures the work, how fortunate she is to have it. In her own words, *'Come sono fortunata.'* Thus, the name I have given it.

"The young woman was the daughter of the noble Gallieri family. After her marriage, she was known here as the *Gräfin von Italien*: Countess Cecilia Karolyi. The portrait is of her."

Vesper glanced at me. Helvitius was too caught up in his account to notice that her eyes had widened for a moment. She said nothing, however, as the loathesome creature continued.

"I conducted certain discreet investigations and deduced that *La Fortunata* was still in Schwanfeld. Over the centuries, the castle had been threatened by the usual petty wars typical among neighbors. The household valuables, each time, were stored away, then brought out again when it was safe to do so. But the portrait no longer figured in the present Karolyi-Walsegg collection. I assumed—I dared to hope—it had been overlooked in the course of these disruptions and restorations.

"When I visited Schwanfeld on the pretext of offering to buy the castle, I explored the basements, the lumber rooms, the storage areas. My assumption proved correct.

"*La Fortunata* had indeed been packed away, forgotten but intact. The late Count Wilhelm had no idea of the treasure in his cellar. As for Sigismund, his interests lie elsewhere. *La Fortunata* is mine at last."

"You went to a lot of trouble for one picture," Vesper said.

"Picture?" cried Helvitius. "To call this a picture is to call the Parthenon a grocery stand, the Taj Mahal a woodshed. I am a connoisseur, Miss Holly. I recognize genius when I see it. Did I neglect to mention the painter's name? It will not be unknown to you."

Helvitius paused a moment, smiling blandly, then added, "Leonardo da Vinci."

Vesper usually takes the most astonishing turn of events in stride. This time, she started. Although it was, I judged, less in surprise than dismay to learn that the abominable Helvitius had possessed himself of a work by this greatest Renaissance master.

"Yes, it is from the hand of Leonardo, beyond any question." The face of Helvitius had turned pink with an avaricious pleasure I frankly found disgusting. He expanded, preening himself as he paced before the fireplace.

"Leonardo's finest achievement, surpassing anything he created before or after. The *Mona Lisa*? A mere daub, apprentice work in comparison. *La Fortunata* far outshines it, eclipses it. Leonardo reached the heights of creation in this single canvas. It is, quite simply, the most superb portrait ever painted.

"Perhaps the subject herself inspired him," Helvitius went on. "Countess Cecilia was a brilliant individual, with a mind as wide-ranging as Leonardo's own. In many ways, Miss Holly, she was not unlike you. There is, as well, one final resemblance. Countess Cecilia died young. So, I regret to say, shall you."

"No! She will not!" I cried. "If my dear Mary is lost to me, then I am lost to myself. My fate, sir, is a matter of indifference. Take your vengeance on me, despicable monster. Release this child. Accept her word that she will make no attempt to bring you to stern justice, much as you deserve it, nor will she try to hinder you in any way."

"Why should I lose one when I have both of you?" replied Helvitius. "Your offer does you credit, but I have neither reason nor intention to accept it."

"Do you think I'd give him my word on anything?" Vesper put her arms around me. "Dear old Brinnie, I wouldn't go along with that offer anyhow. I won't beg him to spare us. That's a waste of breath.

"But—" she added, "there's one thing I'd like. To see the portrait."

Helvitius pondered this a moment. He nodded. "It pleases me to be generous—since it costs me nothing. Few have seen this masterpiece. Few will ever see it again. It will be the crowning glory of my collection, for my eyes alone. Yes, Miss Holly, as a mark of respect for a worthy opponent, I shall permit you a glimpse. It will be your first glimpse of *La Fortunata*. And your last. But it will be a happy one."

Helvitius gestured for his ruffians to follow. I had, finally, extricated myself from the confines of my sheet. Useless freedom! His hirelings kept their weapons trained on us as Helvitius led us from the hall, through a vestibule, and down a flight of steps. Vesper strode along undismayed and eager. Dear brave girl! Threatened with death, she maintained an interest in the finer things of life.

Below, at the entrance to one of the storage rooms, Helvitius motioned for us to step inside. He struck a match to a torch he took from one of the sconces and held it high to illuminate the chamber.

The room was jammed with barrels, packing cases, all the useless and forgotten impedimenta of the household. Atop one of the barrels lay a large cask of Drackenberg cheese.

"*La Fortunata,*" said Helvitius.

Hearing this, I could only suppose the fellow had gone out of his wits, driven mad by the poison of his own villainy, if he mistook a cask of cheese for a Leonardo da Vinci. Nevertheless, he laid one hand on the cask with a caressing gesture, then raised the lid.

"You understand, Miss Holly, while the painting is legally mine by purchase, there is one small inconvenience. Drackenberg has a tiresome law forbidding removal of art treasures from the country. The portrait obviously figures in that category. Therefore, it must be taken out with absolute discretion."

"Smuggle it out, you mean," said Vesper.

"A crude term but essentially correct," said Helvitius. "I foresee no difficulty. *La Fortunata* will soon ornament my collection at my principal estate in— Ah, never mind where. Did you know, Miss Holly, that the Emperor Napoleon hung the *Mona Lisa* in his bedchamber, where he could observe it morning and night? With *La Fortunata,* I shall do likewise."

"Poor Cecilia," muttered Vesper.

Until now, Helvitius had exposed only the wheel of cheese. As we watched, puzzled, he lifted it out.

"I devised this container myself," he said. "You will agree it is very convincing. It gives the appearance of a full cask. Drackenberg's cheese is excellent, but hardly a national treasure. Whereas, here in the false bottom—"

He undid the inner wrappings to reveal an oblong, unframed canvas nestled in the bottom of the cask.

"Behold," he said, "*La Fortunata* herself."

Helvitius has never distinguished himself by telling the truth, nor did he do so in this instance. That is to say, he told less than the truth. He could not have done otherwise, for the reality surpassed all his claims. The words *priceless* and *masterpiece* were pallid understatements.

Despite the inappropriate setting and the flickering light of the torch, there could be no question: Vesper's deduction had been correct. Here, indeed, was the portrait represented in the scene displayed in Count Wilhelm's gallery. As Vesper had assumed, exact though it was, the copy did no justice to the original. It would be inadequate merely to say that Leonardo's portrait conveyed the living presence of Countess Cecilia. It did that and more. Fresh as the day it had come from the master's brush, it radiated a life of its own.

Description is futile. Whatever Helvitius had paid to acquire this masterwork, he had paid too little. Even Philadelphia's titans of art—the magisterial Peale, the sublime West, the incomparable Doughty—would have flung themselves to their knees in humble adoration.

Vesper had been studying the canvas carefully. She

straightened up and folded her arms. Helvitius glanced at her.

"Are you satisfied now, Miss Holly?"

"Is that your Leonardo?" Vesper shrugged. "I'm sorry."

~ **16** ~

Vesper turned away from the cask. "At least you have a fortune in bauxite."

"Miss Holly, you astonish me," said Helvitius. "From one of your intelligence and culture, I expected a more appreciative observation. I show you a masterpiece and you speak of mineral deposits?"

"All right," said Vesper. "It's—interesting."

"Interesting?" cried Helvitius. "You find nothing more to say?"

"Knowing you're going to kill us," replied Vesper, "I can't work up much enthusiasm over what you call a Leonardo."

"What do you imply?" snapped Helvitius. "You dare to claim this is not a da Vinci?"

"If you like a picture, does it matter who painted it? An original, a clever forgery—it makes no difference."

"Outrageous!" exclaimed Helvitius. "You dispute my judgment?"

"I wouldn't dream of it," Vesper answered mildly. "You're the connoisseur. But I always thought Leonardo lived in the fifteenth century."

"Of course he did." Helvitius narrowed his eyes. His face darkened. "What are you hiding? You have information you are keeping from me. Be warned, you will not conceal it for long. You will beg to reveal all you know."

"I don't know anything at all," Vesper protested. "I was only thinking about Perkin."

"What are you saying?" cried Helvitius. "Perkin?"

"Fine chemist," said Vesper. "You must know about him."

"I do," Helvitius retorted. "I have had much correspondence with him in England. He accepted a number of my suggestions regarding bichromate of potash. What has he to do with this?"

"I understand he's done brilliant work with coal tar," said Vesper. "He practically started the synthetic dye business. Less than twenty years ago. That's hardly fifteenth century.

"I'm no expert. You are," Vesper went on. "But I don't think Leonardo would have used a nineteenth-century artificial color. Of course, he was always ahead of his time."

"There is no artificial color in this painting." Helvitius snapped his jaw shut. A faint twitch played over one side of his face. "I have examined every inch of it."

"I'm sure you have," said Vesper. "But—did you only see what you wanted to see? When you have time, after you get rid of us, take another look."

"*La Fortunata* a forgery?" Helvitius shook his head.

Yet his air of arrogant confidence faded a little. Pale blotches appeared on his cheeks. He looked as if he were experiencing the first hints of seasickness. "Impossible!"

"That's your opinion," said Vesper. "You're entitled to it. I'm sure it's genuine," she added soothingly, "if you say so. The brushwork in the folds of the drapery is fine, really. But it's amazing what they can do with coal tar."

"The pigments are natural. Coal tar? Ridiculous!" With a growl, Helvitius bent closer to the portrait.

"Shine the light from the other side," Vesper suggested. "Here, I'll hold it."

She obligingly took the torch from the hand of Helvitius, who continued to squint at the canvas, muttering to himself.

I had been following Vesper's comments with growing interest. William Henry Perkin, that remarkable young Englishman, had made some of his most important discoveries when he was a lad scarcely older than Vesper. It astonished me that even Vesper's sharp eyes had been able to detect his synthetic products in one sweeping glance. I tried to join Helvitius during his scrutiny. Vesper pushed me aside.

The dear girl, in fact, moved so quickly that no sooner did I understand her intention than she had already accomplished it.

In a sudden, rapid motion, she set the torch to the skirt of Helvitius's dressing gown.

The garment burst into flame. Helvitius, too absorbed in examining the canvas, remained unaware of the combustion. After a few seconds, however, he whirled around with a roar, clawing at the blazing robe.

The villain's outcries brought his henchmen. Vesper threw the burning torch at the head of one, who dropped his rifle to fend off the shower of sparks.

"Get the painting!" cried Vesper.

The dear girl's life, not a fraudulent work of art, was my only concern, and I pushed her bodily from the storage room. I had a glimpse of the second ruffian trying to strip off his master's flaming dressing gown while Helvitius attempted to roll on the floor. At cross-purposes, their endeavors did little to relieve his condition.

I dragged the still-protesting Vesper down the passageway. Behind us, Helvitius was bellowing and cursing his hirelings and us alike. One of the ruffians had set off after us. A bullet sang past my ear as we raced up the steps.

The wretch was gaining on us. We plunged into the nearest chamber, only to be confronted by a dozen armed men, rifles raised. In the desperate hope of seizing a weapon, I flung myself on one of them. I staggered back, half stunned by the impact.

It was a reflection. We had blundered into one of Count Wilhelm's eccentric amusements: a maze of mirrors.

Glass shattered as our pursuer fired at us. One of Vesper's images disappeared, but the dear girl herself was at my side. As bewildered as ourselves, the ruffian was uncertain of his targets. Another mirror shattered and fell in jagged pieces.

"This way!" cried Vesper. "Don't look at the reflections!"

She hauled me through what could have been mistaken for another mirror. By now, the second ruffian had joined his comrade, and following them came Helvitius, sooty, robeless, but no longer in a state of combustion.

Vesper darted through the great hall and out the doorway into the courtyard, hoping to gain the drawbridge and make for broken country. A bold but futile attempt, for a hasty backward glance showed me the hirelings had paused to take aim at us.

At that moment, from around the corner of the main building, trotting as fast as his legs could carry him, appeared Pognor and, with him, straining at their leashes, a pair of large dogs. Vesper is more familiar with canine breeds than I am; I could identify them only as a variety of shepherd, but they looked as bad-tempered and snappish as alligators.

Pognor hesitated an instant, blinking at the scene before him. Whether he had misunderstood the order by Helvitius regarding the kennels, or whether he had grasped our plight and fetched the animals to assist us lay beyond speculation. Confused though his thoughts might have been, one thing he clearly realized: The *gnädiges Fräulein* was in mortal danger.

Shouting a command, the old retainer dropped the leashes. Hackles up, snarling and barking, the dogs leaped at the ruffians, who tried to fend off the teeth tearing at their arms and legs. Pognor, clapping his hands, gleefully urged them on.

Given that moment of respite, we raced over the drawbridge and sped across the meadow and into the woodland. Vesper's goal was to find protection in the deepest part of the forest, but the trees grew too sparsely in the immediate vicinity of the castle. We could only scramble up the rising ground, clambering over rock faces and mossy boulders, hoping for some better refuge.

Vesper sighted the heaviest underbrush and plunged into it. I begged her to let me catch my breath, but she dragged me farther until, at last, we crouched behind a thick screen of bushes.

"Good old Pognor," said Vesper. "I hope he has sense enough to get away from Schwanfeld. Helvitius won't be very pleased with him."

She peered through the bushes. "I'd really like to go back there."

"What can you be thinking of?" I cried. "Risk falling into that scoundrel's clutches again?"

"I guess we shouldn't take the chance," Vesper said reluctantly. "But it sticks in my craw, Helvitius with his hands on Cecilia's portrait."

It was, I pointed out, hardly worth risking our necks for a mere forgery. Though Helvitius had gained a fortune in precious bauxite, we could be satisfied that his pride had been devastated by a fraudulent da Vinci.

"It isn't," Vesper replied. "It's real. Leonardo painted it, no question. Helvitius was right. It's a priceless masterpiece."

"What of Perkin?" I exclaimed. "The artificial color? You saw for yourself—"

"No, I didn't," said Vesper.

"You told a falsehood?" I was shocked. No doubt the dear girl was justified, considering what would have happened to us. She had saved our lives. But at what cost to her principles!

"I didn't lie to him," said Vesper. "Not exactly. I only asked a few questions. He did the rest by himself. The portrait's genuine, and I'm not going to let him get away with it. But I'll have to think about that later," she went on. "The first thing is to find Aunt Mary. She's not in Schwanfeld. I'm sure of that."

"Then what has he done with her?" I cried. "He would not say if she was alive. Dear girl, I must fear the worst."

"No, you mustn't," said Vesper, as I put my head in my hands. "She's alive. Helvitius told us so. He didn't mean to, but he did.

"Remember what he said: Why should he lose one of us when he had both? Think, Brinnie. *Both.* If Aunt Mary had been in the castle, wouldn't he have said 'all three'? Besides, if I know Helvitius, he'd have been very happy to tell us Aunt Mary wasn't alive. He'd have gloated over it. So, I say: Wherever she is, she's all right. For the moment.

"But there's more to it. I'm beginning to see what he's planning. Part of it, anyway. We'll need help. We can't stop him on our own, and we can't do anything here. It's going to happen in Belgard."

"Dear girl, what can you possibly—"

Vesper motioned me to silence. She cocked her head and listened intently for a moment. "The same ones? Others in the kennels? Either way, he's set the dogs after us."

CHAPTER

~ 17 ~

"Did they get our scent from those sheets we were wrapped in? They must have." Vesper stood and glanced around. "All right, Brinnie, we can't sit here like a couple of scared rabbits and wait to be rooted out."

She rummaged in her pockets. "I hope I didn't lose my Baedeker. No—it's here."

"What use is that?" Despite Herr Baedeker's admirable thoroughness, I doubted that his little volume would include advice to fugitives.

"I'm looking for a map. They can't track us in water. If there's any kind of stream"—she studied one of the pages—"Schwanfeld and vicinity. No. We'd have to go too far upland. We want to keep toward Belgard."

By now, I clearly heard what Vesper's sharp ears had already detected: the deep baying of a hound. Vesper scrambled out of the underbrush and ventured to climb up a rocky incline. I joined her as she crouched and shaded her eyes, scanning the open countryside below.

In another few moments, one of the ruffians came into sight. His comrade, presumably, had been in no condition for the task. Even this one looked much the worse for wear, with a hastily bandaged arm and a torn shirt.

The fellow was leading—rather, he was being pulled along by—a brindled monster that looked, even at a distance, the size of a Shetland pony. My heart sank. It appalled me to consider that members of the canine breed, faithful and obedient servants, could allow their natures to be so corrupted and themselves turned into vicious tools of villainous masters. The sight of this hound, slavering and straining at the leash, eager to seek us out and sink its fangs into us, reinforced my preference for felines.

I could not prolong my musings. The ferocious creature had picked up our trail and, snuffling and belling, was making implacably for our hiding place.

Vesper calmly took a last glance at her Baedeker and replaced the book in her pocket.

"No help for it, Brinnie. We'll have to double back and get closer to the Belgard road. We can try to outrun them.

"I don't see Helvitius," she added. "If my guess is right, he's busy with something else."

I had, meantime, been taking stock of our predicament. So far, at least, only a single hound had been set upon us. To me, our course was clear and I hurriedly conveyed my thoughts to Vesper.

"Dear girl, we must separate," I told her. "They cannot track us both at once. Make your way to Belgard. At the same time, I shall circle around—"

"No, you won't," Vesper broke in. "You'll stay right with me."

"I shall join you when I can," I insisted. "In this, you must trust my judgment."

"I do," Vesper said fondly, putting an arm around me. "I trust you to do something noble and end up doing something silly. Brinnie, I don't want you out of my sight."

Vesper stripped off her cloak and ordered me to do the same. She bundled up the garments and tossed them as far as she could in the opposite direction.

"That should put them off our track for a while."

She beckoned me to follow as she moved swiftly through the undergrowth, staying just below the ridge before quickly turning downward in a path that would skirt the castle.

It was now well past noon, and I was chilly without a cloak. Drenched with perspiration from my exertions in keeping up with Vesper, I found myself shuddering uncontrollably in the crisp autumn air.

Vesper's face was flushed and tightly set. For all the dear girl's magnificent vitality, I feared that she, as well as I, could not long stand the pace. If the relentless hound had discovered our abandoned cloaks, the ruse had not delayed the creature as long as Vesper might have hoped. The continual baying grew closer.

"Try to stay ahead of them till nightfall," Vesper called to me as we pressed on through the lower stretch of woodland. "In the dark we'll have a better chance to give them the slip."

This was not to be. Rather than lose ground by staying

within the shelter of a long line of trees, Vesper chose to make a dash across an open meadow. Behind us, the hound set up a frenzied yelping. It was no longer our scent that drew him, but the clear sight of us racing over the field.

His keeper, too, had seen us. Sure of his prey, he made no attempt to run after us. Instead, he unleashed the animal, who needed no urging to streak forward at such a rate that he appeared to fly.

While we succeeded in leaving his keeper far behind, the hound gained on us yard by yard. Vesper can run like an antelope, if need be, but her two legs, already wearied, would soon prove no match for the canine's four.

To me, our only hope lay in finding the tallest tree and climbing it. Heading for the woods, I signaled this course of action to Vesper.

"No!" she cried. "Brinnie, no! We'd be trapped there!"

Further discussion was not practical, since our chance for any kind of escape had vanished. The animal's blood was up; nothing could divert him from his purpose as he bounded across the field.

I gasped in horror and despair, and flailed my arms to attract the beast's attention to my own person. But baring fangs capable of ripping out a victim's throat in an instant, the hound voiced a triumphant bay and made straight for Vesper.

CHAPTER

~ 18 ~

Vesper is always kind to animals, and deeply concerned for their well-being. Confronted, however, with a charging hound whose only object was to tear her limb from limb, she could hardly be expected to display her usual sympathy and understanding. As she braced herself for the monster's attack, I could not say she was terrified—it is not the dear girl's nature to give way to terror—but she was as close to displaying that emotion as I have ever seen her.

For myself, I was too paralyzed by the sight of this huge, slavering creature—an instrument of destruction rather than a useful domesticated animal—to do more than stare helplessly. Therefore, I did not immediately see a small figure sprinting past me.

"*Rawnie!* This way!"

Her long skirts kilted up, her black braids flying, Mikalia seized Vesper's arm and pulled her toward the fringe of woods.

Zoltan was only a few paces behind the girl, moving quickly despite his bulk. To my disbelief, he ran forward to face the raging hound. *Barossan* he might be, but his behavior convinced me he was also a lunatic. Seeing a new and unresisting prey, the brindled monster's eyes blazed and he bared his fangs in an expression of bloodthirsty pleasure.

The Gypsy calmly squatted down, motioned with his hands, and made peculiar whistling, sniffling noises. I would have turned away, unable to bear the sight of Zoltan being chewed to pieces. But I could not believe my eyes; nor, I am sure, could Vesper.

The hound skidded to a dead stop. While Zoltan kept on with his odd sounds, the beast stood as if frozen, tongue lolling, massive head cocked to one side.

The *barossan* now stepped softly toward the animal, whose tail had begun wagging as joyfully as a house pet greeting its long-absent master. The Gypsy knelt and, wrapping one hand around the creature's muzzle, whispered in the animal's ear; then, to my further astonishment, he gently nipped the beast on the scruff of its powerful neck.

When Zoltan straightened up, the hound hunkered obediently at his feet, paws outstretched, eyes filled with nothing less than devotion. The *barossan* made a gesture with his hand, fingers spread wide, and turned back to us. The hound did not budge.

"Rawnie," Zoltan said to Vesper, who had been too caught up by his accomplishment to express her gratitude. "Horses you may know about. Dogs, you still have much to learn."

But now the animal's keeper hove into view at the far edge of the clearing. Taken aback to see the ferocious animal reclining on the ground instead of tearing us limb from limb, the ruffian finally regained enough of his wits to unsling his rifle.

The shot rang across the meadow. Happily, fatigue influenced our pursuer's aim, and the bullet ripped harmlessly through the foliage.

"It works with dogs, not people," said Zoltan. "Move along, *rawnie.*"

As our would-be captor stood undecided whether to fire again or further exhaust himself by running after us without benefit of the hound, Zoltan hurried us through the woods. A little distance further, two unsaddled and unbridled horses cropped the turf. The *barossan* heaved himself astride one of them. Vesper swung up behind him, her arms clasped as far as possible around his sizable girth. Mikalia mounted in front of me and set the horse cantering after Zoltan.

We went swiftly along a forest track, Mikalia too intent on keeping pace to provide much in the way of conversation or explanation; and I, equally intent on staying aboard the jolting steed, was not inclined to ask questions.

The light had begun fading rapidly. My attention concentrated mainly on gripping the bare back of the horse with my aching knees, I was aware only that the forest thinned a little as we pressed along the downward-sloping path. Soon, in the gathering blue twilight, the lanterns of the caravan glimmered ahead.

At the arrival of their *barossan* and ourselves, Rosika, Tibor, and the rest of the *kumpania* ran to greet us. Vesper, along the way, had already told Zoltan what had befallen us; now, she was obliged to repeat her account to the overjoyed Gypsies. Zoltan, thumbs hooked into his sash, took a nonchalant attitude while Vesper described his confrontation with the hound; for all that, the *barossan* was not displeased with himself. His barrel chest swelled somewhat beyond its usual capacity, and he beamed fondly at Vesper.

"You see, *lavengro*," he explained, finally turning his attention to me when Vesper concluded her tale, "Mikalia and I thought it best to follow you soon after you left us. We thought our horses might be useful to you on the way back. But we lost time going to the *vardo* for them. So, we came too late to help you at the spa. There was no sign of you by then, but Mikalia made her way into the kitchens, as if to beg food. She learned that two very sick *gorgios* had been carried away in an ambulance. We followed you. To the *rom*, your track was clear; we had no trouble seeing it." He shrugged. "It was simple enough. I only wish we had reached you sooner."

"We still have to get to Belgard as fast as we can," put in Vesper, disentangling herself from Rosika's embraces.

"Then why do we stand here wasting time?" returned Zoltan. "Do you want to talk or be on your way?"

Putting Tibor in charge of the rest of the caravan and ordering him to follow without delay, the *barossan* motioned for us to climb atop his own *vardo*.

"You can stay on the roads," Vesper said, as we started for the capital. "No use trying to hide now. Anyhow, I don't think Helvitius will be watching. He has something else in mind. We aren't important to him now."

129

"If the horses tire," put in Mikalia, who had insisted on coming with us and who had been clinging devotedly to Vesper, "I can *chore* some fresh ones along the way."

Vesper thanked her kindly, but was more fascinated by Zoltan's taming of the ferocious hound. As we rattled along under a bright moon, she questioned him about it.

"How can I tell you, *rawnie?*" Zoltan replied. "Explain what we *rom* know without knowing? You want me to put it in words or write it down in a book? That cannot be done. You travel with us and you shall learn for yourself, without anyone teaching you."

Mikalia, meantime, had gone to sleep, her head on Vesper's shoulder. My own head began to nod. Worn out by what had been an extremely trying day, and by my anxiety for Mary, I dozed off in spite of myself.

It must have been almost dawn when I opened my eyes with a start to find us rattling across the bridge to the Albertine Palace. Zoltan, following Vesper's instructions, had avoided the path through the Sommerwald and, thereby, saved us many hours of travel.

Ritterhof Square was now fully bedecked with flags and bunting, the wooden scaffoldings completed. With so many other things to occupy my thoughts, I had forgotten that the first of the outdoor celebrations would start today.

"That's why I was in a hurry," said Vesper. "We still have a chance. But there's a lot to do. First, I have to see Duchess Mitzi."

Zoltan reined up at the palace gate. In ordinary circumstances, the arrival of a Gypsy *vardo* at such an unseemly hour might have presented difficulties. The sentry, however, recognized Vesper and complied with her demand to rouse the grand duchess immediately.

130

By the time we were escorted to her apartments, Her Highness was up and waiting for us. She still was in her night-robe, her hair bristling with curlpapers. Yet, in this costume, she looked more formidable and dragonlike than she did even in her full regalia. The curlpapers alone would have been enough to inspire awe and apprehension.

Vesper, however, cast all formalities aside. "Get Inspector Lenz as fast as you can," she said abruptly, before the astonished Maria-Sophia could question her. "I'll explain it later."

"Your Highness," I put in, "we have failed. Mrs. Garrett is not to be found. We must begin our search again."

Duchess Mitzi simply stared at us. Meantime, one of the apartment doors had opened.

Fully dressed and in perfect order despite the early hour, Mary walked into the room.

ᴥ 19 ᴥ

"Brinnie, you look perfectly awful," said Mary. "Wherever have you been? And the dear child—you've led her into some scrape or other, that's plain to see."

It lies beyond my ability to describe my sensations at our reunion. Though I took exception to her holding me responsible for our condition, Mary's observation was justified. What a bedraggled picture we must have presented as a result of our ordeals. Even Zoltan and Mikalia looked the worse for wear. No matter, we were all safe and sound. Embracing Mary at that happy moment, overcome as much by astonishment as by joy, I could hardly begin to ask an explanation of her presence.

"But—but, then," I stammered, "you were not kidnapped as we supposed?"

"Of course, Aunt Mary was kidnapped," Vesper put in. "I think it happened just as we guessed it did: the wagonload of mineral water, those thugs hauling her to Nymphenbaden. The rest Aunt Mary can tell us herself."

"They were disgusting creatures," Mary added, after confirming that Vesper's analysis had been correct. "Altogether coarse and unmannerly, which is to be expected. Criminal pursuits do not attract a better type of individual. One of them had the effrontery to sit on me until the wagon was out of the city. They trussed me up like a parcel amid carboys of Nymphenwasser, most uncomfortable."

"I had to believe you got away," said Vesper. "I wasn't sure how or when."

"Dear girl, you knew that Mary escaped?" To say that Vesper never ceases to amaze me is not empty rhetoric but sober truth. "How could you?"

"I didn't know," Vesper corrected. "But the more I thought about it, the more I hoped I was right. First, Aunt Mary wasn't at Nymphenbaden. Second, she wasn't at Schwanfeld. Third, Bibi and Helvitius acted very cagily, as if they were hiding something. Why? Because they really had no idea where she was. So, one way or another, she probably had escaped. It was the only thing that made sense to me."

"You were exactly right, dear child." Mary beamed at her. "Had you, Brinnie, applied the same clarity of thought, you would have realized it. Dear Brinnie, how could you ever have imagined that I would allow myself to be a helpless victim? To be abducted? Manhandled? And do nothing about it? That sort of treatment is entirely unacceptable. If I'd had my handbag, those ruffians would not have carried me off in the first place.

"However, they did leave me unattended in the back of the wagon, and I was able to loosen the ropes around

133

my feet. I could do nothing about my bound hands or the gag forced upon me, but I was quite able to jump out of the conveyance at my earliest opportunity. The intelligence of those brutes was not of the highest order, so they kept on their way, none the wiser.

"I began walking toward Belgard," Mary continued. "Though I hardly presented a dignified appearance, a kind gentleman in a cart stopped to help me. He was a photographer, returning from a country excursion. He drove me to the palace. His studio, by the way, is near our hotel. He indicated a desire to take my photograph at a more convenient time.

"I have been here ever since," Mary concluded. "We had no means of reaching you, so we could only wait and hope for the best. I repeat, Brinnie, that I am slightly disappointed that you believed me less than capable of taking care of myself. And yet"—Mary turned her shining eyes upon me and embraced me again—"my dearest Brinnie, I am very glad to see you. But I would like to know what you have been doing all this while."

"Not much," said Vesper. "Not as much as Helvitius and Bibi did to us."

She explained what had happened as briefly as she could. Maria-Sophia, listening closely, eyed Vesper with growing respect and affection. At the end, the old woman put her arms around her and said with gruff fondness: "That's quite a tale, child. Blazing dressing gowns, ferocious dogs—"

"Ask her about trying to drown my *kumpania*," put in Zoltan. "On second thought, don't ask."

"None of that's important now," said Vesper. "Thanks

to Helvitius, King Rudolf has an easy job of taking over Drackenberg. The bauxite deposits are worth a fortune to your whole country. But they won't do you any good if Helvitius has his way."

The duchess shook her head. "Those, child, are my concerns."

"Mine, too," said Vesper. "You told me the country needed good solid prosperity. And what about everything you wanted to do for your people? I won't let you miss that chance.

"And that's not all," Vesper went on. "Helvitius with his hands on a priceless da Vinci? The portrait belongs to Drackenberg—and the rest of the world, too—not locked up in his bedroom. No, Cecilia's going to stay here. If I can do what I have in mind."

At this moment, Inspector Lenz arrived, once again roused from his bed. "Miss Holly, I am relieved to see you and the Herr Professor safe and sound, but I am beginning to believe you have decided I am never to enjoy a full night's sleep."

"You'll sleep better afterward," Vesper told him. "Right now, there's no time. You need to send a couple of officers to Nymphenbaden and arrest that sawbones Tiezor. And somebody should go to Schwanfeld Castle to make sure Pognor, the caretaker, is all right. As for Bibi— since he's related to Duchess Mitzi, there's not much you can do."

"Relative or not," Her Highness burst out, "collar him anyway. I'll deal with that wretch myself!"

Lenz, bewildered, spread his hands. "Fräulein Holly, I have not the remotest idea what you are talking about."

"You will," Vesper said. "Zoltan, Mikalia, and I are going to headquarters with you. Brinnie," she added, "you and Aunt Mary stay here. I don't want you underfoot. Then come to the train station. At noon."

"Dear girl," I cried, "what are you going to do?"

"For one thing, have a talk with Inspector Lenz," replied Vesper. "For another, go marketing. And I'll drop in on that photographer, too."

"Photographer?" I exclaimed. "But—why?"

"To have my picture taken, of course," said Vesper.

❧ 20 ❧

Vesper hurried from Maria-Sophia's apartments with Zoltan, Mikalia, and Lenz in her wake, all equally puzzled.

Much as I would have wished to accompany her, I knew better than to interfere with the dear girl when she has something in mind. And, with my dear Mary safe, I confess that bauxite deposits and Leonardo da Vinci were of secondary importance.

Yet, despite Mary's calming presence, Vesper's absence turned me uneasy. Taking leave of the duchess, Mary and I went to our own chambers. I knew I should rest, but even though exhausted, I found sleep difficult, and all the more so as the morning wore on.

Around eleven o'clock, anxious about the dear girl, I saw no point in waiting until noon. I urged Mary to set off with me now. We had ample time to go on foot from the palace to Ritterhof Square.

What should have been an easy stroll turned out to be the opposite. The outdoor festivities had already begun. As Mary and I crossed the bridge, we were nearly engulfed by a brass band in full uniform, blaring away on tubas and trombones, with a dozen glockenspiel players hammering away for all they were worth. Mary found this colorful and entertaining, but I had to clap my hands over my ears and, even so, was practically deafened by the time we had jostled our way to the square.

Spectators overflowed the stands. A number had even climbed the lampposts for a better view. At the far side, bystanders observed a crew of balloonists preparing their brightly painted aircraft for its jubilant ascension. In other portions of the cobbled expanse, provincial dancers cavorted, slapping their boot soles, whooping in competition with a choir of yodelers, they themselves determined not to be drowned out by an orchestra of handbell ringers. In liveliness and enthusiasm, the scene came close to matching Philadelphia's inspiring observance of our Glorious Fourth.

The railroad station was equally crowded. The outbound train to Carpatia stood at the platform, carriages ready to receive passengers. Mary peered around a circle of bystanders.

"Brinnie, is that not the little Gypsy girl?"

Indeed, to my astonishment, Mikalia was engaged in dancing a vigorous *tanana*. The spectators clapped their hands and threw coins into the tambourine at her feet. Why the girl had chosen this of all times to display her abilities, was incomprehensible to me.

At that moment, someone plucked my sleeve. It was one of the porters, in visored cap and blue smock. I pulled away, assuring him that Mary and I were not passengers and had no baggage requiring his services.

"I wish you hadn't come so early," muttered Vesper. "Stay out of the way. Don't go butting into things."

"Dear girl, what are you—"

"Brinnie, will you be quiet?" Vesper turned to Mary. "Act as if you're hiring me. Don't gawk. The train's leaving soon. I'm watching for Helvitius."

"In such a crowd?" I replied. "Mikalia has half the station blocked."

"Yes. That's the way I want it," Vesper said under her breath. She led us down the platform and halted under the roof of a baggage shed. Urging us to keep out of sight within the shadows, Vesper leaned on one of the carts and idly picked her teeth with her thumbnail. Beyond the shed, a porter trundled a wheelbarrow. Something about him struck me as familiar.

"Zoltan?" I started forward.

"Let him be," ordered Vesper. "It's all arranged. We won't have long to wait."

By now, the railway guard had started slamming shut the carriage doors. The clock in the tower pealed the first stroke of twelve.

"Blast it, where's Helvitius?" Vesper frowned anxiously. "Did I guess wrong? Lenz has his people all around. Mikalia's got the crowd blocking that end of the station. Zoltan's keeping watch, too. We're bound to catch him. He has to take this train. Unless"—she hesitated, dismayed—"unless I miscalculated everything. If I did, there goes our only chance."

The locomotive had already built up its head of steam. The engineer gave a couple of high-pitched shrieks of the whistle. If the dear girl expected the momentary arrival of

Helvitius, I feared her plan, whatever it was, had gone sadly awry.

"No!" Vesper cried. "I'm right! Lenz should be ready. Don't his men see? There!"

Vesper's eyes were fixed on one of the train conductors, a bulky fellow in cap and uniform.

"Helvitius!" I gasped. "The scoundrel!"

Striding along the side of the train, with an air of purpose and authority, came the villain himself. He halted at the step of the first carriage and calmly took out his pocket watch, studying it as if to verify the exact hour. He nodded, appearing satisfied that all was in order.

Another instant and he would swing aboard the train, already in motion. I understood what I must do.

"Brinnie—no!" cried Vesper.

I did not hear her. That is, I did not wish to. My blood had come to a boil at the sight of my dear Mary's abductor. Vesper sought to restrain me, but I tore away and raced for Helvitius. Somewhere, a police whistle shrilled.

I paid no heed. The vile monster started at the sound, then turned to confront me. I commanded him to stand his ground, but the arrogant wretch only gave me a scornful curl of his lips. Then he realized that Lenz's officers were hurrying toward him from the other end of the station.

I threw myself in front of the step to block his access to the moving carriage, and would have grappled with him then and there.

With a growl, he sprang away from my grasp and plunged through the crowd. Instantly, I was at his heels. Scattering bewildered onlookers, Helvitius sped toward Ritterhof Square. Behind us, the train chugged out of the station.

Vesper called after me, but I dared not slacken my pace. The scoundrel had already gained the middle of the square, flinging aside the yodelers and bell ringers, and sending the dancers sprawling.

To my dismay, I understood his goal: the balloon.

Its gaudy bag, fully inflated now, hung above the wicker basket straining at the mooring rope. The crew had not yet boarded. Helvitius brutally struck them aside. In one swift motion, he cast off the rope and sprang into the basket. As the balloon lurched upward, I was no more than a foot away. I seized the rim and shouted for the crew to help me bar its flight.

Too late! I found myself suddenly borne aloft, legs dangling and fingers gripping the basket. I struggled to clamber aboard as Ritterhof Square fell away below me. I glanced up to see the abominable Helvitius grinning. With cold-blooded determination, he began to pry my fingers loose.

Despite all my efforts, my grip at last gave way. The balloon leaped skyward.

"Bon voyage," Helvitius called, waving a cheerful farewell.

As the vile creature soared into the clouds, I plummeted to earth.

❦ 21 ❧

The majestic rule of gravity, the imperious law of falling bodies, must be experienced to be truly appreciated. I recall only a wild giddiness, a horrible sinking in the pit of my stomach as I plunged downward, flailing arms and legs as if that would save me from the inevitable collision with Ritterhof Square. My abrupt arrival there eliminated further sensations.

I awoke in the certain and comforting knowledge that I had been granted my heavenly reward. Two angels were bending over me: one with calm gray eyes, the other with marmalade-colored hair.

Vesper smiled at me while Mary laid a soothing hand on my brow. I was not in the celestial realm but in our bedchamber in the Albertine Palace.

"You're fine, Brinnie," said Vesper. "You didn't break anything."

"Thanks to the dear child," Mary added. "She practically caught you in her arms."

"Not really," Vesper said modestly. "You mainly fell on the yodelers. But they're all right too."

"Helvitius!" I cried, trying to sit up amid the bed-clothes.

"I won't say he went off trailing clouds of glory," replied Vesper, "but he's gone. According to Baedeker, the prevailing wind here blows west. By this time, he's probably landed somewhere in Carpatia."

"The wretch has defeated us!" I exclaimed. "Not only does he have title to all of Drackenberg's bauxite, but the painting— Dear girl, what of *La Fortunata*?"

"I guessed right about that," said Vesper. "Cecilia's portrait was on the train."

"The train left." I groaned. "I saw it."

"Yes, right on time," said Vesper. "That part couldn't have worked better."

My head spun. I feared I had suffered a concussion. I could understand nothing of Vesper's remarks, nor could I account for her calmness in the face of such a disastrous loss.

"It's very simple," Vesper said, "once you put all the pieces together. We knew Helvitius was going to smuggle out the portrait. He told us so. I suppose there must be a dozen passes in the mountains along the border. But he'd gone to a lot of trouble hiding the picture in that cask of cheese. He wouldn't lug it through the Carlomanians. He didn't have to."

"He did the easiest thing," Vesper went on. "He sent it express to himself in Carpatia. Right on the train."

"The train must be stopped!" I exclaimed. "We must telegraph ahead before it crosses the border!"

"Brinnie," Vesper said quietly, "there's something you ought to know. You've been unconscious for two days. The train's already in Carpatia."

"Then the portrait is hopelessly lost!" I clutched my reeling head. "If Helvitius has landed safely—as he must have done, for he has the devil's own luck—he need only go to the express office and claim it. But how could he know it would be on that train?"

"He saw it put in the baggage car. There's only the noon train to Carpatia. He knew the express company was bound to have the cask of cheese on it. He wouldn't want to let something so valuable far out of his sight, so I was certain he'd be on the train, too. He likely bribed one of the trainmen to get hold of the conductor's uniform."

"Indeed, then, the monster has outwitted us."

"Brinnie, don't you remember when we came to Drackenberg?" said Vesper. "Our heavy baggage was inspected ahead of time in Carpatia. The customs officers made an inventory of all the items, then sealed them in the baggage car.

"It's the same when you go from Drackenberg to Carpatia. The cask of cheese was inspected and stowed away.

"One thing I didn't expect," Vesper went on, "was you chasing after Helvitius and letting him escape in a balloon. Otherwise, we'd have got him and the portrait both.

"Inspector Lenz simply used his authority to unseal the car. Then Zoltan and I, dressed as you saw us, went and took the cask, and Lenz sealed the car again.

"But the cask was already listed on the inventory. That's why I had to go to the market. I bought a real cheese in an ordinary cask. Zoltan carted away the false-bottomed one. I replaced it. When Helvitius claims the cask, he'll get exactly what the inventory says: cheese."

"And a priceless Leonardo is in the hands of a wandering Gypsy?"

"Can you get out of bed?" Vesper asked. "It's about time you did, anyway."

With Mary's help, I climbed to my feet. Vesper led me to the parlor of our suite. She pointed to the wall.

There hung *La Fortunata*.

It had been set in the simplest of frames, which only enhanced its magnificence. Countess Cecilia smiled back at me. The beauty of the portrait, truly Leonardo's masterpiece, took my breath away. Also, in my view, Cecilia looked more Vesperish than ever.

"There she is, Brinnie," Vesper said with quiet satisfaction. "Duchess Mitzi complained that nobody visited her art museum. With Cecilia there, can you just imagine? She'll bring people from all over the world—scholars, students, tourists. I think she'd be happy about that."

As I went to examine the canvas at closer range, Duchess Mitzi came thumping into the apartment.

"Up and around, are you?" Her Highness remarked. "I hope you feel better than you look."

"Brinnie knows all that happened," said Vesper. "Wait—no, he doesn't." She turned to me. "Too bad you couldn't have been with us in Ritterhof Square when Duchess Mitzi gave her speech. It was marvelous. You should have heard them cheer when she told them about the bauxite deposits."

I could not see why that should be an occasion for rejoicing.

"Surely," I said, "those resources belong to Helvitius, wherever he may be. The scoundrel bought the Schwanfeld estates. Deplorable though it is, he does, in fact, own them."

"I own them," said Her Highness. She motioned with her stick toward Vesper. "The child knows our laws better than I do."

"When I was looking through those books in the library," Vesper explained, "I found some volumes of old statutes. One of them says that whoever conspires to commit a felony forfeits all possessions to the crown. Trying to smuggle out a national treasure is certainly a felony, as Inspector Lenz agrees. So, Duchess Mitzi has every right to take all that Helvitius owns here. He spent a fortune—for nothing.

"That law dates from the fifteenth century," Vesper added. "It's as if Countess Cecilia had reached out and collared Helvitius herself."

"The monster will not profit from his ill-gotten gains," I replied, "but neither will Her Highness. Dear girl, you forget that Helvitius alone has the formula for extracting aluminum. So he told us and, in this case, I fear he spoke the truth for once."

"Don't worry about that, Brinnie. Science is knowledge, and nobody can own it all by themselves. Not for long, anyhow. Helvitius gave away part of his secret when he bragged how much he knew about electrochemistry.

"That's the best clue," Vesper went on. "Duchess Mitzi will hire the best scientists in Drackenberg. I'll have a talk with them. Once I tell them to look into using electrochemistry, that will point them in the right direction.

They'll figure out the formula soon enough. If they have any trouble, I'll be glad to help them."

"Child," said the duchess, "you've helped us more than I could ever have imagined. But it's not going to happen that way. Not exactly. I'm not hiring any scientists or anyone else."

"You have to—" Vesper began.

"I said *I'm* not doing it," replied Maria-Sophia. "I'm going to found a whole institute of scholars and scientists. After that, they'll be on their own. Whatever they discover will go for the benefit of Drackenberg.

"That's not all," Her Highness continued. "As for Schwanfeld and everything in it, I'm turning it over to the nation. That old fellow, Pognor, can stay on as custodian. There'll be plenty of tourists to keep him busy.

"I'm giving Cecilia to the nation, too," she said, "along with the art museum and the opera house. They won't belong to me, they'll belong to all of Drackenberg. And so will the profits."

"That's wonderful," Vesper exclaimed, delighted, "but you'll have a lot of organizing to do."

"Not I," said the duchess. "I'm leaving all that to my new cabinet, my new council—and my new parliament. I did chew over what you said to me. You'll see a lot of changes in Drackenberg. There's no way Rudi will take over. The people won't let him.

"Of course, when I turn into an ancestral portrait, somebody will have to succeed me." Duchess Mitzi eyed Vesper closely. "I wish you were one of my relatives. There'd be no question who'd be grand duchess after me.

"But we'll manage somehow. I'll leave it to the new government to choose. Only one thing I'll insist on," she added, with her old dragonlike glare. "It won't be Bibi. In any case, he's gone off who knows where. He won't show his face in Drackenberg again."

Vesper, naturally, was overjoyed by Duchess Mitzi's declarations and wanted to know more details. For myself, I wished to learn the answer to a question that remained to puzzle me.

"Dear girl," I said, "on top of everything else you had to do, why did you want your picture taken?"

"When you make a plan, Brinnie, you have to allow for something going wrong. In case Helvitius got away—which he did—and went to claim his shipment—which I'm sure he will—I put the photograph in the cask of cheese."

Vesper grinned wickedly. "When he opens it, he'll have a little something to remember me by."

Next morning, when I was able to get around without too much difficulty, Mary, Vesper, and I went to the deer park. Zoltan's *kumpania* was packing up, making ready to go south. Mikalia saw us first and came running to throw her arms around Vesper. A few moments later, the *barossan* himself arrived.

"So, *rawnie*," said Zoltan, "you've come to wish us *bahtalo drom*."

"As I promised," said Vesper.

"You don't need to." Zoltan sucked on his gold tooth and cocked an eye at Vesper. "Not if you come along with us. You're practically one of the *rom* already."

"Come with us," pleaded Mikalia. "I'll teach you *duk-*

148

kering—telling fortunes. Or anything you want to know."

"Tell fortunes?" Zoltan snorted. "That's nonsense for the *gorgios*. We *rom* make our own fortunes. Sometimes not so good, but sometimes not so bad. What does it matter? No, you'll learn something better: how to be free."

"I've already learned some of that," said Vesper. "I know you pay a high price for it."

"Why not?" exclaimed Zoltan. "It costs what it costs. But, *rawnie*, we'll never give it up."

"I know you won't," said Vesper. "Neither will I. But I have my own kind of freedom, and I want to keep it."

"Do you mean you'll leave us?" Mikalia's lips began to tremble. "No. How can you do that?"

"She can't," said Zoltan. "There's a part of her that's Gypsy as much as any *rom*."

"Yes," replied Vesper. "And that part will always be with the *rom*."

"Ah well, then," Zoltan burst out, "do as you like. What can it matter one way or the other?" He blew out his breath, shrugged his shoulders, and turned away for a moment. Finally, he glanced at Vesper again.

"A part? Yes, and I take that part with me." He put his big arms around her. "For the rest—*bahtalo drom, rawnie.*"

"*Bahtalo drom,*" murmured Vesper. "*Bahtalo drom,* Zoltan *barossan.*"

149

CHAPTER

❧ 22 ❧

We did not see the rest of the jubilee celebrations. For one thing, I did not feel quite up to any more yodelers and bell ringers. For another, Vesper was busy most of the days, conferring with a number of chemists and metallurgists to discover what Helvitius had believed to be his secret formula. By the time Vesper was convinced they were on the right track, I was fit enough to travel. Mary, I suspected, would gladly have stayed a little longer. But I was anxious to be home and, I believe, so was Vesper.

We exchanged fond farewells with Duchess Mitzi. I think Her Highness was still casting around for a way to keep Vesper with her in Drackenberg, so I was happy to be on our way before she could find some pretext short of offering Vesper the throne itself. Not that Vesper would have accepted. The dear girl would have made a splendid grand duchess, but the position would have required her to leave Philadelphia. Naturally, she would have refused.

In Strafford, Holly's papers were in the same state of

disorder as when I left them. I plunged into them as best I could, with the usual lack of headway. Mary was busy resettling us after the disruptions that always result from an extended holiday.

Vesper herself was very much occupied. She took up plunking her banjo, which had been long neglected. For the most part, however, she spent her time in her laboratory. She had promised to conduct some of her own experiments and communicate her findings to the scientists in Drackenberg.

She said nothing of our near-fatal experiences, and frankly, I was glad she did not. I happily put them out of my thoughts, and was sure Vesper had done likewise.

The days, by now, had begun drawing in. Most of the autumn leaves had flamed and fallen. Walter, the man-of-all-work, had raked them into long windrows, and Moggie scuttled through them as if they had been arranged especially for his amusement.

One afternoon, requiring her advice on some detail of Holly's old correspondence, I went to her laboratory. Instead of finding her amid her test tubes and beakers, I saw that she was standing by the open casement, in her hand the gold amulet Zoltan had given her.

The sharp scent of burning leaves filled the room. Vesper took a deep breath of that pungent aroma.

"It reminds me of Zoltan's campfire," she said half wistfully, watching the blue haze drifting through the orchard. "I'd almost expect to see lanterns swinging back and forth on the *vardos*."

"Be glad we're all safely home, and comfortably so," I replied. "Now you have other things to think about."

"As a matter of fact, I do." Vesper gave an odd little smile. "How did you guess?"

I did not reply. It is, I have long realized, quite impossible to guess what goes on in the dear girl's constantly active mind, so I made no attempt to speculate. She would tell me soon enough.